Grace wishes Billy would talk about her the way he talks about his plane.

Grace studied the craft. "It's the first time I've been this close to an airplane. It doesn't seem very sturdy." Just a bunch of wires and wood covered with fabric. Who'd want to go hundreds of feet off the ground in such a thing?

"She's a dandy. She'll get me where I want to go." He pounded heavy stakes in the ground and secured the plane to them with ropes. "Wouldn't want anything to happen to this baby. Tomorrow I'll take her up again and scout around. When people see there's an airplane in the area, I'll be getting all sorts of jobs." He tied the last rope and straightened, his gaze lingering on the aircraft. "I always figured a Curtiss Jenny Canuck is the prettiest machine they ever made." He gave the plane a fond look. "A real beauty."

Grace's mouth tightened. He had said more sweet words in the past fifteen minutes than she'd heard in the last year, and it rankled that they were for the benefit of some tin bucket. . . .

In bed later, she snuggled close to him. He pulled her to his side. "I am so happy. This is my dream come true."

After he'd fallen asleep, Grace faced the wall. If only he had meant her when he spoke of his dreams coming true, rather than his airplane.

LINDA FORD draws on her own experiences living in the Canadian prairie and Rockies to paint wonderful adventures in romance and faith. She lives in Alberta, Canada, with her family, writing as much as her full-time job of taking care of a paraplegic and four kids who are still at home will allow. Linda says, "I thank God that He has given me a full, productive life and that I'm not bored. I thank Him for placing a little bit of the creative energy revealed in His creation into me, and I pray I might use my writing for His honor and glory."

Books by Linda Ford

HEARTSONG PRESENTS
HP240—The Sun Still Shines
HP268—Unchained Hearts
HP368—The Heart Seeks a Home
HP448—Chastity's Angel
HP463—Crane's Bride
HP531—Lizzie
HP547—Maryelle

Grace

Linda Ford

Heartsong Presents

Dealing with feelings of inadequacy is a universal issue.
I hope this story helps people see past false expectations
and comparisons to the fulfillment of a relationship with God.
This relationship blesses all other relationships.
To that end, I dedicate this book to my daughters,
Yvonne, Dionne, Christine, Jolene, Tania, and Kelsey.
You all have such incredible strength and beauty.
May you learn to walk in that knowledge all your days.

A note from the Author:
I love to hear from my readers! You may correspond with me
by writing:

> **Linda Ford**
> **Author Relations**
> **PO Box 719**
> **Uhrichsville, OH 44683**

1-59310-061-2

GRACE

Our mission is to publish and distribute inspirational products offering exceptional value and biblical encouragement to the masses.

All Scripture quotations are taken from the King James Version of the Bible.

All of the characters and events in this book are fictitious. Any resemblance to actual persons, living or dead, or to actual events is purely coincidental.

PRINTED IN THE U.S.A.

one

Alberta, Canada, 1920

Twenty-year-old Grace Marshall waited as her husband helped the liveryman unload the wagon. It didn't take long to pile the trunks, the bed frame, and the stove in the middle of the yard, and then the liveryman tipped his hat back and scratched his forehead and studied the house. "I 'spect it looks better inside than it does out."

His dubious tone did nothing to relieve the sinking sensation in Grace's insides at the enormity of what they faced.

Billy, never one to admit a difficulty, handed the man a fistful of coins. "We'll have it right soon enough, you'll see."

"Don't know." The other man shook his head. "No one has lived here since the Martin family moved out. What was left of them. Poor folk. Flu pretty well wiped them out. 'Course they weren't the only ones around here to be struck hard." He wagged his head sadly. "We were hit hard by the flu. Over three thousand Albertans died of it. On top of losing more than sixty thousand in the war. It was bad."

"War," Billy said in his matter-of-fact way, "is hard on everyone. I heard over eight million people died in the war and two, three, perhaps even four times as many in the Spanish flu that struck around the world."

"Say, didn't I hear you're a veteran?"

Billy smiled. "I flew in the war."

"Ya don't say! Shoot down many of them Huns?"

"Thirteen planes and two zeppelins." Billy's chest expanded until Grace wondered how his buttons stood it. Not that she minded. She was proud as could be of her war hero.

The man shoved his hand toward Billy. "We need more young people like yourselves." He pumped Billy's arm. "If you folks be needing anything, you just give old Len at the livery barn a holler. I'll be right glad to help you out." He studied the pile of belongings. "Don't look like much for starting a new life."

Billy laughed. "We don't need much."

Grace studied the stack. It had seemed so much when Billy organized its delivery to the train. Now it looked pitifully inadequate. She resolutely turned to watch her husband as he spoke to Len. Billy never failed to see the possibility in a situation—a chance for adventure. Not for the first time, she wished she could so readily view the future. But she dismissed her anxieties. As long as she had Billy, she'd be just fine. "I'm sure we'll manage," she assured the wagon driver, fearing his face would crumple in with worry. "But thank you for your kind offer. We'll keep it in mind. Won't we, Billy?"

"Certainly. It's most kind of you." But already he had turned toward the house, his eyes running up and down its length, seeing, no doubt, the possibilities, whereas she viewed it with the same sensation she'd have if she swallowed a stone.

"Well, I'll be on my way then." Old Len clambered onto the wagon. "All the best to you folk."

Billy barely let the wagon begin to rumble away before he took Grace's hand. "Well, here we are. What do you think of it?"

Warmth raced across their joined hands, driving away the doubts. Grace laughed at her worries. "To be quite honest, I'm surprised the place is still standing. Are you sure it's liveable?" She said it jokingly, although her heart quivered inside her chest. This dubious house was all the protection she could look forward to.

"The man who rented it to me said it would take some work. That's why he gave it to us so cheap. But he assured me it was nothing major." He grinned at Grace. "How bad can it be?"

She drank in the confidence in his dark eyes, letting it drive deep into her soul and soothe her. She gave a quick grin as she thought of how her sister would react if she knew Grace was moving into a rundown house, miles from the nearest city, in the wilds of western Alberta. "If only Irene could see me now."

His grin tipped up on one side. "She'd be surprised at how adventuresome you've become."

"I should say she would. So would Father. To think they didn't think I could even manage to cross the ocean by myself."

A frown flitted across his face. "It still rankles that they didn't trust me to take proper care of you."

"I've told you before not to take it personally. They've always coddled me. I think Father would have refused to let us marry if he'd known we weren't staying in Toronto."

"You won't be needing any more coddling." Without giving her a chance to reply, he pulled her toward the house. "Let's have a look at what we have."

She ignored a shiver of apprehension as they picked their way across the yard over scattered shingles, bits of wood, and a pile of ashes that seemed to have been flung from the doorstep. Billy lifted the padlock, and it fell away in his hand. "Guess I won't need this." He pocketed the key and flung open the door. "Behold your new home."

Grace gasped. "It's a ruin." Two broken chairs leaned upside down against a stack of wood. A rusty pail gaped at her. A fluttering of feathers topped some rotted boards. Had some animal killed a bird and eaten it here? She swallowed hard and tried not to think about it. Her feet crunched across the debris, and she stared at round little pellets that she was certain were animal droppings. "It smells dreadful."

Billy stepped around her. "We'll fix it up in no time. You wait and see."

"No time?" She planted her fists firmly on her hips and faced him. "I admit I don't know a whole lot about running a house or fixing things. I admit I've led a rather sheltered life and been spoiled by my sister and father. I'll even admit new challenges frighten me, but Billy, my dear husband, it is now five o'clock in the afternoon. We have no stove set up and no bed in which to sleep." She snorted. "What kind of miracle do you have in mind that will have this mess fixed up in 'no time'? You can't even see the floor."

He tipped back his head and grinned at her. "My, my, but aren't you English all of a sudden?"

She glowered at him. "You know my accent is worse when I'm upset."

"Am I to understand that you're upset right now?"

"Upset would be putting it mildly." She pursed her lips. "When you said we were heading west, I agreed." The alternative was staying in Toronto with his family, and even though she loved her mother-in-law and enjoyed city life, she could not imagine surviving without Billy. "But I naturally assumed we would at least have a place to live."

"No need to be snippy."

"Snippy? I'm not the least bit snippy." Her hot breath puffed through her gritted teeth.

He chortled. "Downright snippy I'd say. About ready to chew me limb from limb." He glanced about the room. "I'm thinking I should arm myself."

She laughed, her anger gone as quickly as it had come.

"That's better. You scare me half to death when you get all snorty like that."

She dismissed his remark with a flick of her finger. "Seriously, what are we going to do?"

"Let's have a look around." He picked his way around debris. "It can't be all that bad."

"Or it could be worse," she muttered, following him to the next room.

A stuffed chair lay with its feet in the air. "Look, a dead chair." She giggled nervously.

"It needs a proper burial." He kicked it and a mouse ran out, scurrying toward Grace.

She grabbed her skirt, screamed in terror, and raced for the door. She didn't stop running until she reached the top of their belongings in the middle of the yard. A sob caught in her throat as she pressed her hands to her face.

"My, my! I had no idea you could run so fast." Billy stood with his arms akimbo. "That was quite a show."

She glowered down at him. "It was not a show, you great clod."

"It was only a mouse. It's probably more frightened than you are."

"I sincerely doubt that."

Billy held out a hand. "Come on, let's get to work."

She allowed him to assist her to the ground so she could face him squarely. "I am not going back in there. I hate mice."

"So do you want me to live in the yard with you?" He shrugged. "Or is it all right if I set up indoors for myself?"

She felt the sparks flying from her eyes. "You. . .you. . . ," she sputtered.

He grinned. "Can't have it both ways."

She crossed her arms over her chest. "First, you go in there and chase out all the mice. Then. . .then maybe I'll go back in. But if I see another mouse. . ." A shudder raced down her spine. "Dreadful wee creatures."

Billy shook his head. "Never could figure out how such a little bitty furry animal could cause such a reaction. Why I had one for a pet when I was a boy. Kept him in a cage when Mother was about, but I really liked best to carry him in my pocket right here." He touched his breast pocket. "Where I could feel his warm little body—"

"Stop." Grace clamped her hands over her ears. "Or I'll never go back in there."

"Aw. I was only teasing."

"It's not a teasing matter."

"You take life too seriously. A little fun makes everything easier."

She turned away without answering. What he said was

true for Billy—life was for fun and laughter. It was one of the qualities that made her love him so intensely, but there were times she wanted to be more serious, more in control.

"You wait here while I go shake the rafters. I'll give you a holler when I've rattled things around enough to have chased away any of those dreadful little critters." He laughed all the way back to the house and slammed the door so hard Grace wondered if it would still be hanging on its rusty hinges. He bellowed through the house, "Be gone, you vile creatures. I can't have you scaring my fine little wife. I want her to help me clean out this mess so we can have our supper in our fine little house." He banged doors and kicked walls.

Grace grinned at his nonsense.

"And I want to get my bed set up right here in this room." It sounded like he stomped on the floor. "And I want my fine little wife right here beside me in my bed warming me and pleasing me."

Grace felt her cheeks warming. She could never get used to his brash way of referring to their lovemaking. For her the pleasures of being man and wife were intensely private. For Billy it was something to shout to the earth. She shook her head. Was it possible two people could be more opposite than she and Billy? No wonder Father had asked her several times if she was certain she knew what she wanted.

"Grace." Billy's voice rattled through the empty house. "Grace Marshall. You can come in now."

She tiptoed toward the house.

"You hoping they won't hear you?" Billy grinned at her futile exercise.

She peered down her nose at him. "One can never be too cautious, you know."

Billy hooted. "How very British of you." He drew his mouth down into a severe frown. "Care for a cuppa, Dear?"

His brown eyes twinkled, such a marked contrast to his wretched frown that Grace couldn't help laughing. "You can practice all you want, but you'll never have the proper bearing."

She pulled herself very straight and tucked her chin in. "Would you be so kind?"

Billy chucked a lump of dirt at her. "You do that so well, my dear."

"It's all in the proper bearing." She caught the lump and threw it back.

He ducked. "Here now. That's no way for a proper English miss to act." He imprisoned her in his arms. "What would your father say to such behavior?"

She wrinkled her nose. "I'm afraid there's a lot about my present situation he wouldn't approve of."

"You don't say?" Billy leaned back to stare into her face. "I'm sure I don't know what you're meaning."

"As if you don't. Didn't you assure him you were taking me to a fine house in the city where I would have servants and all the proper conveniences? Not to the back of beyond."

"What I said was my parents live in Toronto in a fine house. I never said anything about my plans."

"No, I suppose you didn't."

He grew serious for a moment. "Truth is, I didn't have any plans. At first, it seemed there would never be anything but the war. And when it finally ended, I guess I thought I would go back and pick up my old life. It just wouldn't work, that's all."

"I know. You tried." They'd spent almost a year in Toronto with Billy working alongside his father and brother, John. She'd have had to be blind not to see he wasn't settling into civilian life. His announcement that he was heading to Alberta to return to flying shouldn't have surprised her. But it did. She'd chosen to ignore the warning signs.

He dropped his arms, releasing her. She shivered. It felt so much safer with his arms around her.

"Now let's get at this job."

"I suppose you're right." But she hesitated as he trod up the steps and back into the house.

"Grace. You coming?"

"Of course." Only by clamping down on her bottom lip

could she still the panic rising at the thought of coming face-to-face with another mouse.

Already Billy was scooping up garbage. He faced her, his arms full. "I'm going to carry this out and burn it. Bring another armload, will you?"

She stepped aside to let him pass, grateful he didn't look at her and guess her distaste. "One thing good about being pampered," she muttered to no one in particular, "is never having to do this sort of mucking out." Billy couldn't hear her, nor did she want him to. He would only grouse about her being spoiled. So dusting her palms on her skirts, she grabbed a broken board with the tip of her thumb and forefinger.

"Great lot of good that'll do."

She shrieked at Billy's voice so close behind her and dropped the board. "Don't do that."

"Do what?" His grin did nothing to convince her his surprise hadn't been intentional.

"Here, you do this." She nudged the board toward him with her foot.

"And what will you do?" He loaded up his arms without so much as checking under anything.

"How can you bear to do that?"

He gave her a puzzled look. "Do what?"

"What if there's a mouse nest under there?"

He shrugged. "Grace, when you've had to share a trench with rats as big as dogs and wonder if they'd chew your nose off in the night—"

She held up her hands. "I've told you before. I don't want to hear about it."

He gave her a hard look. "Poor Grace. Don't spoil her day with any hard truths." He paused at the door. "Grace, someday you're going to have to accept life isn't all roses and tea."

"That's not fair. I'm not exactly blind, you know. I've seen the realities of life." But he didn't hear her, or if he did, he chose to ignore her. "I've even experienced a few," she muttered. After all, she'd left home and sailed across the ocean.

And she'd left the comforts of city life to accompany him to the back of beyond. That was about as much hardship as she cared to deal with. She wasn't one to go borrowing trouble.

Billy clomped back in the house. "Grace, aren't you going to help at all?"

"Of course I am." She gingerly picked up two boards and, ignoring Billy's exasperated sigh, marched outside and threw them on the blazing fire.

Billy followed, dumped his load on the flames, and rubbed his soiled hands on his pants. "It was the barn that convinced me this was the right place, and I'm glad to see it's going to be big enough to work in. I wonder what it's like inside." He took a step toward the structure, then pulled up. "Guess we better get the house looked after first."

She followed him back inside, as reluctant as he, but for a different reason. The thought of a mouse hiding under each piece of garbage made her wish for the pampered life she'd known until now.

Hours later, Billy shovelled out the last pile of dirt.

Grace looked around the room. "I don't see how we're going to get sorted out enough for tea. Or even bed."

Billy arched his back. "It's a bigger job than I thought, but what else can we do but keep at it?"

"I'm tired. Couldn't we go back to town? Perhaps buy a meal and a room for the night?"

Billy thought a moment. "We'd have to walk. You up to that?"

Grace groaned. "I'm about beat."

"Then what?"

She wilted like a coat falling from a hook. "I don't know. What exactly did you buy?"

"Canned goods." He dug into the pile of goods and retrieved several cans. "We have beans." He set the first can aside. "Beans." He retrieved another. "Or beans." He tried again. "Or we could have peaches."

"Jolly good."

He jabbed his knife into the top of a can and pried it open. "Help yourself. Or do you want me to find a fork?"

"I wouldn't mind being able to wash up."

"Time to try the pump." He unhooked a pail from the top of the pile and marched toward the iron pump close to the house. After priming it with water they'd carried with them, he got a burst of rusty water that soon gave way to a clear stream.

Grace plunged her hands into the gush of water. "This is lovely," she murmured, scooping her hands to her face and sucking in the cool water.

Billy washed up and drank heartily before the two of them settled down to enjoy a can of beans and share a can of peaches.

"Tomorrow we'll get the house ready to move into," Billy said.

"Where will we sleep tonight, Luv?"

"Tonight we will sleep under the stars." He tilted his head back to study the sky. "Look at that sky."

"Very nice. But where will we sleep?"

He sighed. "How about a mattress on the ground?"

"It seems wrong."

"What would be wrong about it?" Billy sounded displeased.

"I was never allowed to sleep outside as a child. Father insisted it wasn't proper. It was so drummed into me, I can't help wondering if we'd be doing something. . ." She tried to find words to explain her reluctance. "Well, something improper."

"Grace, my dear proper English gal, where do you suppose the settlers slept as they moved into this land? There were no fancy roadhouses, not even a friendly neighbor with a house to share. For that matter, where do you think all the soldiers slept when they took their turn at the trenches? Did you think there was an inn lurking just over the ridge for their convenience?"

Stung by his sarcasm, she mumbled, "No, of course not. But those were men—soldiers."

"The settlers brought wives and daughters with them." He held up a hand. "And before you entertain the notion they were lower-class folk, think again. Some high-and-mighty people came west." His expression softened. "Besides, doesn't it excite you to spend our first night together here sleeping in the yard? Take a look around you."

She did as he said.

"Do you see any neighbors who would be shocked if they knew?"

"I guess not." Now that she let herself think about it, the idea did carry a certain allure. She laughed. "All right. Let's do it."

"That's more like it." He grabbed the mattress. "Help me with this, would you?"

They carried it to a grassy spot.

"Do you know where the blankets are?"

"I do." She found the right trunk and pulled out an armload, spreading them on the mattress.

A little later, she lay beside him, staring into the sky.

"Do you realize," Billy began, "this is the first time we've been on our own since we were married? First, we were with your family. Then there was the trip across the ocean." He grunted. "You sleeping with the women and me bunked in a hole with the rest of the men. It was dreadful."

"So you've said." She laughed. "About a million times."

"What a way for newlyweds to get to know each other."

"Then we moved in with your family. Not that I minded. Your mother was so nice."

"Just like the mother you never had. I know. You've said it about a million times."

Grace turned on her side to look at him. "It was hard to say good-bye to her."

"I guessed that's what all those tears meant."

She punched his arm playfully. "You'll never let me forget that, will you?"

"I guess I should be grateful you chose to come with me rather than stay in Toronto with my family."

"We're married after all."

He didn't answer, and she wondered if he had the same

sense of being married to a stranger as she. She lay back beside him. "It will be different."

"Different? What? How?"

"Being on our own. Having to learn to do everything. I know nothing about running a house." The two-week period after Billy announced they were moving had been consumed with getting ready, leaving her little time to learn all the things she didn't know.

"I guess it will be a little different having to eat burnt food," he teased.

She chuckled. "Who says it will be burnt? Maybe it will be half cooked."

"I guess that would be different too."

"Do you think you can put up with me learning at your expense?"

"I expect I'll survive."

"I hope so." She longed for assurance, yet she feared if she told Billy how overwhelmed she felt, he would laugh at her. Or say it didn't seem like a big thing to him. As if that somehow should make her feel better.

His deep breathing beside her warned her he had gone to sleep. The fire still flared. In the dancing golden light, she studied her husband. His black hair gleamed; his fine nose threw a shadow across his face; his well-drawn mouth was soft in sleep. As handsome as ever.

She felt the deep stirrings she had whenever she allowed herself to examine her feelings for him. He made her feel so needy, so desperately needy. It was a sensation she didn't know how to handle. It alarmed her. If only he would say again how much he loved her. If only she wasn't afraid to ask, afraid he would laugh at her fears.

two

A blast of light woke Grace. She opened her eyes and turned toward the sun, red and round, rising above the horizon, heralding morning by flinging ribbons of orange and pink across the gray sky. Birds answered the call, hundreds of unseen birds filling the sky with song. Grace lay on her back, eyes closed, listening to the serenade. Never had she heard such a cacophony of sound. Then it settled to a murmur as if the birds had called their morning greeting to their sundry neighbors and now chattered in their own homes in a quieter, more sedate fashion.

Grace turned toward their house—their house! The idea sang through her. They were finally to have their own home, their own life. Now, she reasoned, she would be treated more as a wife and less as a daughter. She liked the idea.

In the unforgiving morning light beaming past the low unpainted barn, the house looked more forlorn than it had in yesterday's softer evening rays. But she smiled. This was their first home. Anxious to make the place liveable, it was all she could do to lay still.

She knew the minute Billy woke up. His breathing paused, a jolt of energy twitched through his limbs, and he turned over on his back, instantly awake and ready to face the day.

"Well, it appears we survived our first night."

She giggled. "I can't make out if you're happy about this or disappointed. Were you hoping the night would be more eventful?"

"I think I would have slept through most anything." He stretched and sat up. "What first? Food or tackle the house?"

Grace's stomach churned. "Just thinking of having to scour that house makes me feel sick."

He jumped up. "I guess I could get a fire going and make some tea." The flames soon leapt into life. He fashioned a wire across the fire and hung a pot of water to heat.

Grace lay clutching her stomach, trying to keep the nausea down.

"We need something besides tea," Billy mused.

Grace kept her eyes closed. "We really are a pair of babies, aren't we? Neither of us knows the slightest thing about some rather essential skills like cooking. I hope we don't starve to death."

"No need to fear." He rummaged through the supplies. "There's plenty here. The store man said I had everything I'd need. Here's flour." He pointed at a large, cloth-covered sack, then at a smaller one. "And sugar." He grinned at her. "Know what we can make with that?"

She shook her head. "Haven't the foggiest. Any suggestions?"

"I 'spect there's all sorts of things, but don't ask me. Did you happen to bring a cookbook?"

She sat up so suddenly, her stomach protested. "I never even thought of it. Now what are we going to do?"

"We'll muddle through somehow." He turned back to the box of supplies. "You think we can survive on beans?" He held up two cans.

Clutching her stomach, she moaned and lay back down. "I don't think my tummy likes beans. What else do you have?"

"Lots more beans. The man at the store said they were an essential staple."

She groaned.

"Never mind. We'll find something else. Ahh. More peaches. We'll have tea and peaches. How does that sound?"

She sat up cautiously. "Sounds palatable enough."

A few minutes later, they shared a pot of tea and a can of peaches.

"That takes care of breakfast." Billy tossed the can in the fire and stretched his arms high over his head.

Normally she found his energy and enthusiasm catching,

but this morning she could think of nothing she'd rather do than lie down again. The tea and peaches had done nothing to settle her stomach. Beans definitely did not agree with her. "As soon as we get the stove set up, I'm going to make a proper meal."

"Great. What will it be?" His grin was wide and teasing.

"I think I could scramble some eggs."

"Trouble is, we don't have any. The man at the store suggested we buy some hens so we could have our own supply."

Her jaw went slack. "Our own chickens? We're beginning to sound like farmers."

"Too bad it's too late to put in a garden."

Grace stared at him. She had so much to learn.

Billy filled two buckets at the pump. "I'll get some water heating. In the meantime, let's see what needs to be done."

She followed him to the house. The smell inside was overpowering, and she clutched her midsection and moaned.

"What's wrong?" Billy stared at her.

"It's the smell. It makes me feel sick."

"Then let's get rid of it." He grabbed the broom. "I'll sweep the floor, then we'll start scrubbing."

She nodded, too nauseated to speak. He swept through once, shoveling out a pile of dirt, then handed her the broom.

"Give it another going over while I get the water."

With one hand, she took the broom, pressing the other to her stomach, determined not to let the sick feeling get the best of her. Without a backward glance, Billy hurried outside.

Grace tackled the floor, relieved to discover work eased her nausea. By the time Billy returned with hot soapy water and rags, she felt a great deal better and had the floor ready to wash.

Billy stood at the doorway and looked around. "I suppose we should start at the top and work down." He glanced at her and then around the room. "How 'bout if I wash the top of the walls and you wash the lower part?"

"Let's do it."

Three hours later they stood back and surveyed their efforts.

"Not bad," Billy said.

"Not bad," she agreed. The upper walls were dark green, the lower half leathery-looking wainscoting that seemed none the worse for the neglect it had endured. After much scraping and scrubbing, the bare boards of the floor now looked smooth and clean.

"Any idea what we will eat?"

Grace shook her head. "I'm guessing it will be beans and peaches. I suppose if we set up the stove—" Her voice trailed off. "Do you know how to set it up?"

"About as well as you know how to cook on it, though I was given some rather cryptic instructions."

She brushed a loose strand of hair from her face. "We are quite a pair, aren't we? What's the expression?"

"Hardy pioneer stock?"

She laughed. "More like babes in the woods." She cocked her head. "Sounds like someone driving by."

"Or driving in."

"Hello, the house." A man's voice echoed through the room. Billy leapt out the door, Grace hot on his heels.

"Name's Tom Deans," said the youngish man, jumping down and extending his hand.

The woman at his side stood, waited a moment for her husband to help her down, then hurried to Grace. "I'm Nellie. We're your neighbors."

"That's our place right over there." Tom pointed. "Two miles due north." He lifted a box from the back of the wagon.

"We thought you would be busy getting moved in," Nellie explained. "So we brought over dinner."

The smells flooded Grace's mouth with saliva. "How nice," she said. "We were just wondering if we would have to eat another can of beans."

"We haven't got the stove set up yet." Billy chuckled. "Guess you can see that for yourself."

"You'll be needing a hand with that," Tom said quietly.

"First, we eat. We could use the table out here or—" Nellie

smiled gently at Grace. "We could set it up inside. What would you prefer?"

"After all the work we've done getting the kitchen clean, I'd like to eat inside. That is," Grace added, growing doubtful, "if the smell from the other room isn't too overpowering."

"We'll ignore it," Billy said, already taking one corner of the table. Tom took the opposite side.

Grace grabbed a chair and followed.

"This is wonderful," Grace announced a few minutes later as she dug into the stew Nellie had brought. She took a bite of the fresh bread. "I doubt I'll be able to do anything like this."

"Don't you know how to cook?" Nellie's voice was soft.

"Not to save my life."

Tom chuckled. "This ought to be quite an adventure." He grinned at Billy. "Think you'll survive?"

Grace liked Tom immediately with his rolling laugh and dancing blue eyes. He and Nellie were as opposite as day and night: she, pretty and dark, petite, and quiet; he, blond, big, blunt featured, and a little boisterous. She darted a glance at her own husband, contrasting his dark hair and fine features with Tom's bluntness. Billy was handsome to the extreme.

"I'd be pleased to help you learn how to cook," Nellie offered.

"I'd appreciate that."

"I hear you're one of them there flying aces." A hint of awe made Tom's voice deep.

"I flew in the war all right."

"And you managed to return home unscathed?"

Billy shook his head. "I sport a few scars. In fact that's how I met Grace."

Nellie leaned forward, her face alight. "How exciting. Do tell us."

Billy shrugged and looked at Grace. "Go ahead."

"My sister was a nurse in a convalescent hospital in our town. She worked long hours there, leaving me on my own. It was very boring." Grace sighed. "I was supposed to stay away from the hospital."

Billy interrupted. "She was only sixteen. Her father thought she should be spared the horrors she would see there."

Grace nodded. "In my boredom, I would sometimes slip up the hill and wander around. Sometimes I would talk to the soldiers sitting out in the garden." She grimaced. "I avoided the ones who were burned."

"Good thing I wasn't burned," Billy muttered.

"Anyway, I was crossing the lawn when I saw this soldier drop his crutches. He had one leg swaddled in bandages, and I figured he had dropped them accidentally so I hurried over to retrieve them for him."

"I was trying to walk on my leg so I could go back to flying."

"And when I bent to pick up the crutches, he collapsed on top of me." She laughed. "I always say he literally fell for me."

"How romantic." Nellie's eyes had grown wide. "And you got married right away before he went back to active duty?"

Billy chuckled. "Not exactly. Her father about had a fit when he found out we wanted to get married. He didn't mind her bringing home a young Canadian soldier for tea. It was the patriotic thing to do, you know, to entertain the Canadians. But at the thought of marriage—" He shrugged. "I guess I couldn't blame him. Grace was so young. Life was so uncertain. Anyway, he made us promise to wait."

Grace nodded. "We got married after the war ended."

Nellie sighed. "I still think it's romantic. A war bride."

Back east, Grace had quickly learned not everyone welcomed English war brides, feeling they had stolen more than their share of eligible young men.

"And I love your accent."

Grace smiled. "Thank you." Apparently Nellie had no problem with accepting Grace. "How about you two? How did you meet?"

Nellie shrugged. "Nothing very exciting, I'm afraid. Our families lived on neighboring farms." Her gaze softened as it rested on Tom. "We've known each other most of our lives."

"There's something special about that too." In a way Grace

envied Nellie. She would never have that sense of strangeness with Tom that Grace so often experienced with Billy.

Tom pushed back from the table. "We intend to spend the afternoon helping you get moved in."

"That's not necessary," Grace demurred, even as she welcomed the idea.

"Of course it's not, but we want to," Tom said in his blunt way.

"That's right," Nellie added. "What do you want to do first, Grace? Move in the kitchen things or finish scrubbing down the house?"

"I'd like more than anything to get rid of the smell."

Nellie nodded. "Then we'll finish scrubbing first."

With four of them tackling the rooms, the work went amazingly fast, and the front room and two small upstairs bedrooms were soon as clean as the kitchen.

"I'll help you get that stove set up now." Tom headed for the door as he spoke.

Billy sprang after him.

"I could help you unpack dishes or whatever," Nellie offered. "You quite sure you don't mind?"

"Not at all. I'm enjoying the company." They headed after the men. Grace selected several boxes that the women carried to the house. A row of shelves plus the cupboard Billy's parents had shipped out waited for the dishes and cooking supplies.

"Not that Tom isn't good company," Nellie explained. "Only sometimes I wish for a woman to talk to."

"There aren't any neighbors?"

Nellie smiled. "The Welty family lives to the east. About three miles. Then there's the ladies in town. It's not that far, but we don't go often, and when we do, Tom is always anxious to get our business done and hurry home." She paused from unwrapping china plates. "This is the longest visit I've had with a woman since we married."

Grace nodded. Despite Nellie's serenity, Grace could see she longed for a visit. "How long have you been married?"

"Eighteen months." Nellie ducked her head. "We're going to have a little one in a few months."

"How exciting." Grace refrained from saying the idea positively frightened her. How would she cope with a baby when she didn't even know how to make a proper meal? Was it possible to live on beans and scrambled eggs?

"I can hardly wait." Nellie sighed. "I prayed so hard that I would have a baby right away. It seemed to take so long before it happened." She smiled gently. "I guess God knew I wasn't quite ready. It takes time to get used to being a married woman, let alone a mother."

Grace paused from setting supplies on the shelves. "I've been married more than a year, but I still haven't gotten used to it." She lined up a tin of tea and some spices she had no idea what to do with. "I suppose it doesn't help that we've always lived with someone else."

"This is your first time alone?"

Grace nodded.

"Oh my. I guess you'll have a lot of adjusting to do yet."

"What do you mean?"

Nellie looked serious for a moment, then chuckled. "Two people don't become one without knocking off some edges." She shrugged. "Maybe you've already learned this, but I can't imagine me being able to do so if I lived with either set of parents. Nor can I imagine how I would have managed without God's help."

Grace turned back to her task without answering. Nellie talked about God like He was a special friend. Grace hadn't heard talk like that before. But what she said about not being able to get to know each other while living with parents made sense. No wonder she often felt Billy was more stranger than husband. There was so much for her to learn. "Tell me about the community."

"Daystown is a nice place. Real friendly. And growing. Why even since we came there's been another grocery store opened and Rexall Pharmacy. And we have a nice church."

She paused suddenly. "Here I am assuming you are a church goer. Maybe I'm assuming too much."

Grace shook her head. "No, I go to church every Sunday if possible."

"That's nice. I hoped we would share the same faith."

Grace didn't respond as she lined up cans of beans. Suddenly, she giggled. "The man at the grocers told Billy beans were the best staple. I think Billy took him seriously." She added four more cans to the growing row.

Nellie laughed. "Don't think I'd want to eat nothing but beans." She looked into the box of groceries. "What else do you have?"

"A few cans of peaches. Oats, sugar, cornmeal, flour—" Grace lifted out more cans. "Baking powder, soda—what's this?" She held up a square can.

"Corned beef. Another of those staples." Nellie shook her head. "Mr. Tunney certainly outfitted you well, but this looks like a grubstake for a cowboy or a prospector. Most folk eat a little better than this." She leaned against the table as she considered. "Several people go together and butcher a cow. I like to can as much as possible so it lasts."

"I don't know how to do that."

Nellie shrugged. "It's not hard. I'll show you the first time and then you're set."

"I hope so." Everything was easy for those who knew what to do. It seemed to Grace she didn't know how to do anything. "I guess I shouldn't have been so content to let others look after me."

Nellie studied her openly. "I can see why people want to take care of you."

"Why do you say that?" She didn't think her helplessness was quite so apparent.

"With those big, dinner-plate blue eyes, hair the color of golden velvet, and that English complexion. Why, Girl, you look like you should be sitting on a royal throne with servants at your beck and call."

Grace burst into laughter at Nellie's description. She held her hand out in a royal gesture. "How generous of you, but that's not why I've been coddled."

"Then why?"

"I was never a strong baby. My mother was ill following my birth and died when I was an infant. I guess that's why I was sickly. Anyway, according to my sister, Irene, it was a miracle I lived. I suppose they never got over the fear that I might get ill again."

"You're fine now, aren't you?"

Grace snorted. "I'm as strong as a horse and haven't been sick since I was very young. I've had to fight to be allowed to run and play. I suppose I lacked the will to fight for anything more until Billy came along."

"Well, we all have to start someplace." On those practical words, Nellie resumed unpacking dishes.

The men staggered into the house under the weight of the stove and lowered it into place.

"We were looking around," Tom said. "Billy was anxious to see what needed to be done in the barn. He's got an airplane in Edmonton he's going to bring here. He's offered to take me for a ride."

"The barn will do nicely as a workshop." Billy addressed Grace. "I'll be able to do repairs and tinker about."

The men went out, returning with stovepipes and a handful of spanners, and immediately set to work joining pipes and adjusting things.

Nellie had a puzzled expression. "Won't you be needing the barn for your cow and horse and chickens?"

"There's a little pen at the far end where I can put chickens when we get them."

"I said we could spare some milk," Tom added. "Even with the baby, we have more milk than we can use."

Satisfied that everything had been arranged, Nellie returned to her task.

"Let's try it out," Tom said a few minutes later. A fire was soon going in the stove, and Grace set the kettle to boil. "I'm afraid I haven't much to offer except beans." Everyone laughed. "But we can have tea."

"Tom, I put in a tin of cookies if you want to fetch them from the wagon."

"I can't tell you how much I appreciate all this help," Billy said as the four of them sat down for a break.

"Yes, thank you." Grace glanced around the room. "It looks ready to live in."

"We'll help bring in the bed and dresser before we leave," Tom announced.

"And I'll get you started on supper," Nellie told Grace. She stared at the row of cans. "There's lots here, I guess. If you've a particular fondness for beans."

Grace giggled. "We have flour and sugar."

"If you had eggs I could show you how to make pancakes. As it is. . ."

"I'm beginning to suspect we don't have an adequately stocked pantry."

Nellie sighed. "Unless you truly like beans."

Grace wrinkled her nose. "I wouldn't mind them once in awhile, I guess."

"Maybe we should begin at the beginning. I'll help you make a list of what you need." Grace found pencil and paper and began to write as Nellie listed items. "Yeast so you can make bread. Potatoes and maybe some vegetables. I have so much in my garden. Too bad I didn't think to bring some over. I will next time."

As the list grew, Grace's doubts doubled. "I have no idea what to do with all these things."

"I'll come over again in a day or two and give you a few lessons. In the meantime, ask Mr. Tunney for a cookbook. He's bound to have something." She picked up a pail of lard. "How would you like to learn how to make biscuits?"

Under Nellie's capable supervision, Grace soon had a pan of biscuits ready to go in the oven.

"You could open a can of beans or the corned beef to eat along with this. Or you could eat them with syrup. I see Tunney gave you the largest pail available. Anyway, you won't starve. Do you know how to make porridge?"

"Don't you pour oats into something?"

Nellie rolled her eyes. "Close. Here, I'll show you what to do."

The men went back and forth with boxes, a dresser for the bedroom, and two rockers for the front room.

"That's that." Billy dusted his hands against his trousers. "Again, thank you."

"I'll be back first chance I get," Nellie promised.

Amid a flurry of good-byes, the Deanses left. Grace stared after them until the wagon disappeared behind a dip. "That was nice."

"Sure was. I bet it would have taken us three days to do all that by ourselves." He turned toward the barn. "Supper won't be ready for awhile, will it?"

Following his gaze, she smiled. "Supper will be very simple tonight."

"That's fine."

She knew his attention had already gone to the work he wanted to do in the barn. "I'll be busy for awhile getting the bedroom set up. I'll call when the meal is ready."

"Fine." He headed away.

Grace watched his long, easy gait. Everything about him spoke of self-confidence. It was part of the reason she loved him. For him, nothing was too big a challenge. Probably why he was a good war pilot; he loved the risk and excitement. She turned toward the house. It was no wonder he never noticed her reluctance, her lack of confidence. She took a deep breath. He didn't seem to need the reassurance of her love the way she needed his assurances. Nellie's words came back to her. If Nellie and Tom needed time to learn to be man and wife even though they had known each other for years, was it any wonder she felt as if she didn't know who she was or what was expected of her?

As she filled the drawers in the bureau and made up the bed, she heard crashing about in the barn and smelled pungent smoke. Billy didn't intend to waste time getting the barn to rights. When she finished and the biscuits were baked, she walked out to get him, pausing in the open door to watch him. She never got tired of watching him; he attacked everything with such enthusiasm.

He saw her, and a quick smile creased his face. "Isn't this great?" He waved at the pile of straw he'd pushed up in the middle of the floor. "As soon as I clean this out, I'll have room to work. I have a ton of ideas I want to work on. I'm sure if I changed the struts on the wings, I could strengthen them. And if I mount a camera, I could take aerial surveys. Wop May said several companies have been asking about that." He looked past her, out the door. "I can hardly wait to get my airplane and park her right out there. It's been way too long since I've been up in the air." His eyes focused on her. "You'll have to come up with me."

She jerked back. "Me, fly?" She shook her head. "I couldn't. I don't want to."

His mouth fell open. "You're joking. There's nothing like it. Once you've been up, nothing else in life is as exciting. It's like being free for the first time in your life." He nodded. "You'll change your mind for sure when I get the airplane here and you see how beautiful she is."

She narrowed her eyes. When was the last time he'd looked at her with that gleam in his eye and raved about her beauty? Or admired her with eyes burning with such passion? What was so special about a stupid airplane?

Her chin shot up. "Supper's ready." She couldn't seem to help the way her lips tightened. Not that Billy noticed. His dreamy gaze sought the place where his airplane would one day stand. She spun on her heel and marched toward the house.

three

"Good supper." Billy tipped his chair back. "You did fine."

Grace had opened beans and corned beef for him, but biscuits and syrup had been enough for her. "I couldn't have done it without Nellie's help."

"It certainly was kind of them to come help."

"They seem like a nice couple."

"Very."

"Did Tom mention God at all?"

"It came up a time or two, why?"

"Nellie talked like God was a good friend. Like she thought of Him being right at her side. I didn't know whether to be impressed or put off by it."

Billy gave her words a moment's consideration. "Now that you mention it, Tom talked much the same."

"What do you make of it?"

He shrugged. "Maybe it's part of their upbringing. Or maybe they've had some sort of profound experience."

"What do you mean?"

"When I was overseas, there were pilots who claimed they had some sort of mystical experience with God. I remember one fellow who'd been shot and figured he was done for. He said he called out to God and somehow—he said he couldn't explain it—he felt a warm presence with him. All I know is he made it back to the airfield even though his machine was damaged beyond belief."

"Did he act differently afterward?"

"Only in that he talked like God was sitting in the seat next to him. I found it a little annoying after awhile."

"Sort of like Nellie."

"I guess."

"But what do you think of it? Could God really feel that close to someone?"

He took the last biscuit, drowning it in syrup. "Seems strange to me. I figure we're all right the way we are. I believe in God. I believe in salvation, but after that it seems to me God pretty well leaves us to live by the seat of our pants. Seems to me God has little interest in the affairs of man. After all, look at the war, the flu epidemic, and stuff like that. Where is God when that happens? Obviously He expects us to make the best of a bad situation."

"Yes, that seems right to me. But Nellie and Tom are so nice. It's hard to understand how they think the way they do."

"Certainly doesn't make them any less likeable, does it?"

"Not a bit. I liked Nellie right off. And they were so helpful. Nellie helped me make a list of food we'll need to get started." She giggled. "It's a little different than Mr. Tunney's."

"No more beans?"

"Nellie said that was cowboy grub."

He nodded. "Things have fallen into place much faster than I thought they would, thanks to the Deanses' help. I think I'll take the train to Edmonton tomorrow and pick up my plane."

She nodded. Again that gleam of excitement in his eyes.

"Why don't you come to town with me and do the shopping?" he suggested.

Grace quickly agreed.

As soon as the kitchen was tidied up, Billy yawned. "Bed sounds awfully good. I know it's early, but I'm tired."

"I'm not about to argue." Weariness had plagued her most of the day, and she willingly followed him upstairs.

"Everything unpacked and sorted out?"

"Yes. I put your things here." She pointed toward the top drawers. "My belongings are in the bottom. The rest is still in the trunk." She'd pushed it to the end of the bed and draped a plaid robe over it.

"It looks fine, don't you think?" he said as he looked around.

Pleased with how she'd arranged the room and pleased

Billy seemed to appreciate it, Grace smiled. "It does."

He dropped his trousers to the floor and draped his shirt over the bedpost, then crawled between the covers. "This feels good. A bit more comfortable than sleeping outdoors." He opened the covers invitingly. "A lot more private too."

She jumped in beside him, eager for his kisses.

He pulled her to his bare chest. She trailed a finger along his ribs, pausing to trace around the spider-shaped scar near his waist. Beneath the covers, a longer, silver scar went from knee to thigh—reminders of how he had flirted with death during the war. The thought of how she might have lost him in one of his daring forays into enemy territory sent a shudder across her shoulder.

His arm tightened around her. "Not cold, are you?"

"No. Someone must have tiptoed over my grave."

"Boo," he yelled.

"What was that for?"

"Chasing away whoever was tiptoeing over your grave."

His expression grew serious, and he trailed a tickling finger across her lips, then cradled her head, pulling her toward him until their lips met. With one hand at her neck and the other holding her cheek, Grace felt sheltered in his love. She wrapped her arms around him, hugging him desperately.

Later, after he'd fallen asleep, one arm draped over her, she listened to his slow, deep breathing. He'd fallen asleep without saying the words she longed to hear. She stared into the darkness. Why didn't he ever say how he felt? A treacherous thought stole in. Did he not speak of love because to do so would be to lie?

She sighed. There was no point in thinking about it. All it did was make her feel lost and uncertain. But there were times she could barely contain her own feelings; she longed to say "I love you" all day long. So why didn't she? Because, she admitted, something inside would not allow her to do so. Not until he spoke first.

❧

Billy stood at her side as the train chugged into the station. "I wish I could help you with the grub. Keep in mind, whatever you buy, you have to carry."

"I'll try and judge accordingly."

"Here's money to buy what you need." He gave her a handful of bills. "If you need more, Mr. Tunney will give you credit. I haven't made arrangements at any of the other stores yet."

She nodded. Steam puffed incessantly from beneath the train, warning blasts reminding her Billy would soon board the train and leave her alone.

"I'm not sure how long I'll be, but I'll probably be back before dark. There's no need for you to hurry home. Take your time looking around town. Go see Nellie if you like." He paused. "Can you find the way?"

She nodded. The two-mile walk from home was direct enough. And to go to the Deanses' simply meant turning right instead of left at the first road.

Billy hurried up the steps as if he could make the train get to Edmonton sooner by his efforts. He turned to wave. "Have a good day."

"You too." She waited until the train pulled away before she turned toward town.

The station backed onto the main street. Stores of either sandstone or tall board fronts marched up and down the length, giving way to tidy, tree-lined yards. Houses in neat squares along straight streets spread out on either side. Grace hurried down the steps, anxious to explore the town.

Deciding to wait until she was tired of wandering around town before she made any purchases, she examined the inside of every store that caught her attention. After a bit, her steps took her down the side streets. A sign in front of a building caught her attention, and she stared at it.

"Daystown Public Library," she read. Just what she needed. She hurried inside, stopping at the door to fill her lungs with the familiar smells of books and papers.

"Good morning."

She followed the sound in the dusky interior and discovered a bespectacled, plump woman standing between shelves. "Good morning," Grace said. "I'm so glad to discover Daystown has a library."

The woman lowered an armload of books to a table. "Sounds like a confirmed reader speaking. I'm Mrs. Paige, the librarian. Glad to be of service."

Grace stood between shelves, studying the titles. "I had to leave most of my books behind when we moved. You can't imagine how hard it was to choose which ones I must part with. Keep the book of plays or my favorite novel?" She held out her hands as if weighing the decision in each palm. "Be practical and bring a home medicine book, or be romantic and bring a book of poems." She sighed. "A dreadful predicament."

Mrs. Paige laughed. "Maybe we can help ease some of your pain."

Grace nodded. "I believe you can."

"You're that new woman who moved into the old Martin place, aren't you?"

"Grace Marshall."

"Welcome to our community. And especially welcome to the library. I perceive we have found a loyal supporter."

"When it comes to books, I'm very loyal."

Mrs. Paige laughed. "We recently got in fifty new titles. Perhaps some you haven't read yet. What are you interested in?" She led the way to a table where the books stood on display.

Grace picked up one. "There's something about a new book." She lifted it to her nose. "I don't know if it's the ink or the binding, but there is an alluring smell to them." She breathed deeply. "Full of mystery and promise."

"If you're looking for mystery and promise, I suggest this one." Mrs. Paige handed Grace a brown bound book. "It's the story of a man who decided to trek across Africa. I've read it and can recommend it highly."

"I'll take it." She paused. "That is, if I'm allowed to take out books."

"Of course." The librarian bustled toward the square wooden desk next to a potbellied stove. "All you have to do is fill out one of these cards."

Grace filled out her name and address and handed it back.

"You're all set," Mrs. Paige said. "Have a look around."

Grace picked up book after book. "It's hard to decide."

"They'll be here next time, my dear."

Grace gave a rueful laugh. "I know, but it's still hard to narrow it down to what I think I can carry home."

In the end she added two romance novels to the adventure book. As she checked them out, she thought of home. "I don't suppose you'd have a book that will tell me in a few simple lessons how to cook and run a house."

Mrs. Paige chuckled. "I've been married for twenty-five years, and I'm still trying to figure out how to reduce it to a few simple lessons. Or maybe I should say, a few simple steps. But I do have something that might help." She scurried to the far end of the room and held out a weighty volume. "Not condensed, I'm afraid, but I've paged through it a few times, and there's lots of valuable advice here."

"Establishing a Pioneer Home and Kitchen," Grace read. "The title sounds like what I need." She flipped a few pages. "The Basics. Setting Up the Laundry. Bread and Other Essentials. Preserving. Storing Vegetables." She closed the book. "I'll take it and see if I can mangle my way through it."

The librarian patted her hand. "No one is born knowing everything. The one who fails is the one who fails to try."

"I suppose that's right." She bid the older woman goodbye. Anxious now to get home and enjoy her books, she hurried to Mr. Tunney's store with the list she had prepared, and a few minutes later, her bag bulging, she headed down the street toward home. Sweat trickled down her back by the time she stepped in the door and let the bag fall from her shoulders to the table. She sank to the nearest chair, panting.

"I'm grateful I didn't try to carry any more." The room echoed with emptiness. She shivered. She couldn't remember ever having been alone before.

She jerked to her feet, mumbling, "I'll put everything away first." Immediately she promised herself she would stop talking to herself. It was too strong a reminder that there was no one else around. She put the baking supplies on one shelf. The canned beef she'd purchased, she set aside, planning to use it for the evening meal if Billy got back in time.

Mr. Tunney had had two dozen, farm-fresh eggs. "You're really lucky to get these, Ma'am," he'd said as he'd bundled the precious lot into a small box. "I don't often get them in the store except when Mrs. Jackson has extra and she trades them. This is the first she's brought me in two weeks."

Grace understood eggs were a precious commodity until they could get some hens of their own and she took them down to the cellar.

She picked up the instruction book, opened it to the first page, and began to read about the importance of being properly prepared. "It's a bit late to think about preparations," she muttered, forgetting her promise not to talk aloud to the emptiness.

She flipped through a few chapters, glancing at the information, lingering on instructions on how to set up a pioneer kitchen. There were receipts for "mainstay" meals, and she read these with keen interest.

"But I don't have all this stuff."

She mentally marked receipts for biscuits, griddle cakes, and cookies, noted the directions for preparing meat, then pushed the book aside. "I'll study it more later," she murmured. The novels beckoned, and she took the book on top. *The Lady in White.*

"I'll rest a bit, then get to work." She carried the book into the front room, pulled the rocking chair close to a window, and was immediately transported into the world of a young lady in England, who made a habit of wandering around the extensive gardens in a fine white dress. There she encountered a handsome young man who grew to love her. The words of love he spoke to the heroine were vivid and strong.

Grace sighed. How she longed to have her handsome Canadian hero make the same passionate declarations.

A sudden roar made her jump up in alarm. The sound faded slightly, then returned.

She ran outside. An airplane circled the house and tipped toward the barn.

"Billy. He's home." She'd lost track of time and read the whole afternoon.

The airplane bounced on the field next to the barn and taxied to a halt. Billy climbed from the farther back of the two seats and jumped to the ground. "Whooee! Isn't she a beaut?"

Grace ambled toward the barn. "You got home in good time."

"I couldn't wait to get up in the air again." He shouted with laughter. "It's the best feeling in the world. Man, is it good to have an airplane again."

Grace studied the craft. "It's the first time I've been this close to an airplane. It doesn't seem very sturdy." Just a bunch of wires and wood covered with fabric. Who'd want to go hundreds of feet off the ground in such a thing?

"She's a dandy. She'll get me where I want to go." He pounded heavy stakes in the ground and secured the plane to them with ropes. "Wouldn't want anything to happen to this baby. Tomorrow I'll take her up again and scout around. When people see there's an airplane in the area, I'll be getting all sorts of jobs." He tied the last rope and straightened, his gaze lingering on the aircraft. "I always figured a Curtiss Jenny Canuck is the prettiest machine they ever made." He gave the plane a fond look. "A real beauty."

Grace's mouth tightened. He had said more sweet words in the past fifteen minutes than she'd heard in the last year, and it rankled that they were for the benefit of some tin bucket. "It's only a hunk of wood and wires."

Billy looked shocked and reached out to pat the belly of the plane, as if Grace's words could somehow injure the machine. "How can you say that? She's a fine machine. Handles real nice." He gave the airplane a fond look. "You got anything to eat?" But he didn't wait for her to answer. "By this time next week, I bet I'll have more business than I can manage." He grabbed her hand and hurried her toward the house.

"Wop May says the real business is in the north."

Grace almost stumbled. "North?"

"Yup. With pontoons or skis, an airplane can get into places that would take days or weeks to get to by any other means. Can you imagine the possibilities?"

"How far north?"

"He says there's a lot of interest in using planes to get stuff into places like Norman Wells, Fort Resolution, and Yellowknife."

"How far north are they?"

"Way north. Up in the Northwest Territories. Uncharted land. I'll bet it takes a real good pilot to work up there."

"Where do the pilots fly out of?" He sounded like he wanted to pack up and get in the action tomorrow—today if possible.

"Wop says Peace River Landing would be the place to set up headquarters."

They stepped into the kitchen. "I haven't made anything yet. I wasn't sure when you'd return." No need to tell him she'd wasted the afternoon reading.

"I'll wait." He washed up, then sat at the table picking up the book she'd left opened.

She waited, hoping he would comment about her industry, but he shoved the book aside. She knew he hadn't really looked at it.

"Wop says Freddie McCall's doing business out of Calgary."

Grace let out a long sigh. Calgary was closer.

Billy continued. "With Wop and Court operating out of Edmonton and McCall at Calgary, I figure we're pretty well situated about in the middle between the two."

The tightness across Grace's shoulders began to ease.

"Unless we decide to head up north. Now that would be an adventure."

A muscle between her shoulder blades spasmed.

"But for now, I think this is the best place to be."

Grace kept her attention on opening the canned beef, struggling to remember the instructions Nellie had given on turning the block of cold brown matter into a delicious meal. All the while her mind raced. There was no mistaking the note of longing when Billy talked about going north, a thought that turned her insides to a quivering mass.

She'd managed to get a few potatoes and some soggy carrots at the store. She peeled and chopped them, half listening to Billy extol the virtues of the Jenny. Her nose twitched, and she rubbed it. She would never have guessed it possible to be jealous of a machine, but listening to Billy rave about the attributes of his airplane, she experienced a bitter burning in her throat. They even gave the plane a name that sounded like another woman, she fumed.

The meat and vegetables simmered; the kettle boiled. She poured tea. Pressing back the resentment she felt at all the talk of Jenny, she got two teacups. "Would you care for tea while supper cooks?" *Supper,* she thought. *Whatever happened to using good old English names for things?* She thought she'd adjusted to the changes in language, but tonight it rankled to call tea supper. All she wanted was to return to her comfortable way of life where she wasn't expected to cope with meals and shopping and everything.

"How did shopping go?"

His sudden question caught her off-guard. She slopped a bit of tea and mopped it up before she answered. "I found the town library and got some books out." She pointed toward the manual. "Maybe I'll learn how to run a house."

"You'll do just fine. I don't know why you worry about it. I don't."

"You can't possibly imagine how awful it could get. I have

absolutely no idea how to do most of the things mentioned in this book."

"That's probably why the book was written, don't you think? For someone who didn't know what to do."

"I suppose."

"You sell yourself short. Just because Irene and your father led you to believe you were unable to do anything on your own doesn't make it so. You are bright and quick and will do just fine."

"I hope you're right." His words rang with confidence in her abilities; a confidence she wished she shared.

"Did you get what you wanted from the list?"

She nodded. "Pretty well. Mr. Tunney said we were lucky he had some eggs."

Billy nodded. "How would you like to go see the Weltys tomorrow and see if we can get some hens?"

"What does it involve to have hens?"

"Beats me. I was raised in town too, remember? But it can't be that hard if everyone does it."

Grace refrained from saying everyone seemed to know how to cook, but that didn't make it easy. She knew there was no point in saying anything. Billy believed it was easy simply because he said so. She reached for the book. "Maybe there's something in here."

But what she read did nothing to calm her worries. "They say you need a warm chicken coop. It tells about proper feeding, how to tell a setting hen, and how to deal with her." She shoved the book aside. "Makes more sense to me to go to a shop and buy them."

Billy laughed. "Some hen somewhere had to lay those eggs before the shopkeeper could sell them. Besides, where's your sense of adventure? It will be fun to learn all this new stuff."

Grace studied the brown liquid in her cup. Finally she looked him square in the eye. "I'm afraid I don't see it as an adventure. I see it more as a chance to discover how many times I can do something wrong."

"You are really and truly a pessimist, aren't you? I believe if someone handed you a hundred dollars, you'd check to see if it was booby-trapped somehow."

"Well, why would anyone hand me a hundred dollars?"

"Who knows? Besides, it doesn't matter. What I'm trying to say is you don't have to always be looking for something to go wrong. Look at us. We have a pleasant little house. The Deanses are nice neighbors." He sniffed and smiled. "And you're turning into a fine cook." He looked at her long and hard. "I knew the first time I saw you that you had the makings of a good woman." He chuckled. "Didn't you try and keep me from falling on my face?"

She gave a half-hearted smile. "I fear it will be me falling on my face now." And with Billy planning to be gone much of the time, who would there be to catch her?

He shook his head and turned to read about raising chickens. "Seems there's not much I can do to keep you from believing the worst about yourself."

She rose to fill plates with the meat mixture. It did smell quite fine. And later, as she sat across from Billy, she acknowledged it tasted fine too. She should be happy with her accomplishment. She sighed. She was, of course. Only it didn't ease the longing she felt inside. A longing she couldn't even put her finger on, something deep inside ached. If Billy would take her in his arms and declare his love with the passion the hero in her book had, perhaps then she would be able to believe in herself and his love for her. If he would even share a bit of the enthusiasm he expressed over his Jenny.

In bed later, she snuggled close to him. He pulled her to his side. "I am so happy. This is my dream come true."

After he'd fallen asleep, Grace faced the wall. If only he had meant her when he spoke of his dreams coming true, rather than his airplane.

four

At the first sliver of light, Billy jumped out of bed. "I'm going to start work on my airplane." He pulled on his clothes, leaned over, and pecked Grace on the mouth, then hurried out, singing loudly.

Grace wondered what could need doing on a plane that had flown him home safely only a few hours ago. For a few delicious minutes she remained in bed, wishing she had nothing more pressing to do than decide what to wear and what book to read. But breakfast would not magically appear unless she did something more about it than snuggle under the covers.

Pushing aside the warm blankets, she swung her legs over the side, moaning as her muscles reminded her she'd done more walking yesterday than she was used to. If only she had been as active as Irene, who liked nothing better than a brisk march across the fields even after working hard all day. As she pulled on her dress and brushed her hair, she wished she were like Irene in other ways. Irene would know how to run the house, make the meals, and even build a fire in the monster stove. If only Father and Irene had encouraged her to be more useful, if only they'd had the foresight to know she would be needing a few practical skills.

She sighed, wishing she could hide in the bedroom all day. But it wasn't possible. Billy wouldn't be pleased if she didn't make a concerted effort to learn how to do things.

She marched to the kitchen to face the stove. Of course, Billy hadn't thought to start a fire. She supposed she should have been pleased at his confidence in her.

Fifteen minutes later, she had a roaring fire going, and following the instructions in the manual for all good pioneer wives, she boiled water and put oats to simmer.

"I hope you like porridge, Billy Marshall," she muttered, thinking the glutinous mass looked more like wallpaper glue. While it brewed away on its own, she read more of the manual.

"My, this book really covers everything." The section on taking care of odors in the outhouse provided more information than she cared for.

After checking on the boiled oats, she headed outdoors to find Billy.

He stood at the nose of the airplane, a can of paint and a small paintbrush in his hands. "I've christened her. Come and see."

Grace went to his side. Black letters on the fabric read *Gracie Two*.

"Where's Gracie One?" she asked.

"Why that's you, of course." He waved the paintbrush at her nose. "I could paint it on your forehead if you want to be sure."

Pleased at his choice of name, she giggled. "I think I can remember my own name." She tipped her head to consider him. "You haven't called me Gracie since we first met." She bit back the rest of what she wanted to say. *You haven't said I love you since we were married.*

"Is that a fact? 'Cause I think of you often that way. Guess I got used to hearing you called Grace." He turned back to contemplating the machine before them. "Did I tell you how proud I am to be the owner of this fine machine?"

She laughed. "It's surely evident in the way you speak." She looked at him, wanting to drag his eyes from the plane and give her the same adoration. "You know, I could get jealous of this machine."

He laughed as if it were a huge joke. "She's mighty pretty, but she'd be a mite uncomfortable to sleep beside. Downright cold and unfeeling, in fact." He grinned at Grace. "Not at all like you."

Her cheeks burning, Grace turned away. "I came to tell you breakfast is ready." She marched toward the house.

"Great." He hurried after her. "As soon as I've eaten, I want to go through the engine thoroughly. I want everything ready when the business starts rolling in."

He accepted a huge bowl of porridge and poured on canned milk and sugar, eating it eagerly. "You are turning into a fine cook."

"Oh yes, quite."

Billy shook his head. "Gracie, my mother always said a compliment should be received with a quiet 'thank-you.'"

Grace blinked. "I didn't think you meant it seriously."

"I know you didn't." His voice was quiet. "But I did. Perhaps you should listen more carefully to what I say. You might discover all sorts of things you've been missing."

"I don't know what you mean."

"I know. Never mind. I'm heading back to the barn to do some work. I'm hoping the car will be here shortly after dinner."

Grace nodded. He'd made arrangements to buy a car the same day he'd bought the airplane. "Will I be expected to provide the man with a meal?"

"I suppose if he hasn't eaten it would be the hospitable thing to do."

"But I don't even know what to make for us."

"Don't worry about it. I'm sure things will work out."

She stared after him as he headed back to his beloved airplane. Easy enough for him to say things would work out. He was in familiar territory with *Gracie Two* and his tools. Whereas she felt like she'd been thrown in the deep end of the ocean and told to learn how to swim before she drowned.

She hurriedly cleaned the kitchen, then turned to her indispensable instruction book, pointedly ignoring the novel that she longed to finish.

She wanted to prove she could do something more difficult for dinner, but in the end she made a batch of biscuits and scrambled some eggs.

"See, you've made a perfectly good meal," Billy said.

Remembering his admonition, she replied, "Thank you."

"Yet you probably fretted all morning that it wouldn't be good enough."

"Not all morning." After she'd decided it was the best she could do, she had picked up the novel and finished it, ignoring the tug of guilt she felt knowing she should be doing something useful with her time. No doubt Irene would have found a way of hanging curtains in the front room or gone and pulled the straggly weeds lurching against the house. But reading was a far more pleasant pastime.

An hour later, Billy came running to the house. "He's coming. I can hear him. Come on, Gracie. Our car will be here in a minute."

She'd been trying to decide what to make for the next meal and gladly hurried outside. This making meals seemed to be an endless task, she decided.

Outside, Billy stood looking down the road toward town. A small black dot bopped along in a tumble of dust. As it drew closer, she could make out the shape of a car and hear the sound of a motor.

Billy stood with his hands in his back pockets, grinning with all the pleasure of a man about to be given his freedom after a long spell in confinement.

Grace smiled. She couldn't blame Billy for his excitement. Goose bumps raced up and down her arms as she realized they were soon to be the owners of their own automobile.

The driver blared the horn, making Grace jump. Billy laughed and wrapped an arm around her shoulders. "Pretty impressive, isn't it?"

The car drew to a stop beside them, and a dust-coated man stepped down. "She's all yours."

Billy hurried toward the vehicle, calling over his shoulder, "This is my wife, Grace Marshall. I'm going to teach her to drive." He turned to Grace. "This is George Arthur, who sold me the car."

She mumbled a greeting. How could Billy drop a bomb

like that, yet remain oblivious to her shock? Drive? An auto? No. No more than she would fly in an airplane!

"Are you anxious to be on your way, or would you like something to eat?" Billy asked the man.

A quiver raced across Grace's shoulders. If Mr. Arthur said he'd like something to eat, she had nothing to offer him but a raw potato.

"A cold drink of water would be nice, then I have to hurry back to town to catch the train back to Edmonton."

"I'll be glad to give you a ride to town," Billy offered, leading Mr. Arthur to the well.

"I was counting on it."

A few minutes later, with a promise he'd be back soon and they'd have the promised visit to the Weltys, Billy perched behind the steering wheel, Mr. Arthur at his side, and headed for town.

Grace plunked down on the front step and shook her head as the men drove away. One of these days, Billy was going to scare her to death with his sudden announcements. Sometimes she wondered if she'd done the right thing marrying him. But with a shudder, she remembered those long months of waiting during the war, wondering every day if he would get shot down, captured, injured, or—she swallowed hard—killed. She remembered the overwhelming relief when armistice had been declared; how she'd almost burst with joy when he'd walked up the sidewalk to her house and announced he was done with war and could they get married now?

The days had been so filled with activity: getting ready to get married, the paperwork, packing, and getting ready to travel. Then they'd arrived in Toronto and been flung into another round of activity: meeting his parents and brother, John, and sharing the same house while Billy settled back into the family business.

Grace pushed to her feet and went indoors. Only Billy hadn't settled into the family business. Seems having once flown an airplane, it was in his blood. This move to Alberta, where, according to Billy, flying opportunities abounded, would allow him to get back to flying.

Grace brushed back a strand of hair. This move was a dream come true for Billy. For her, it was a little more reality than she cared for.

&

A big horse with shaggy feet the size of dinner plates thundered away as they approached. A baggy, skinned dog with a mournful face bayed loudly and stood in the center of the road.

Billy stopped the car. "Get out of the way, Dog."

But the dog only bayed at them, his voice like a fog horn.

Billy turned to Grace. "You'd think he'd never seen a car before."

Grace laughed. "Perhaps he hasn't." But her attention was on the house and scattered buildings a few yards away: dusty, gray buildings with clutter piled against the walls. Children scattered across the yard, raising puffs of dust before they disappeared from sight. "It appears the Weltys have several children."

From the depths of the Welty yard, a voice bellowed, "Hound, enough racket. Get yer sorry self back here."

The dog gave one more defiant woof, then shuffled away, his loose skin following in waves.

"Whoe'r be there, come on in and make yerself known."

Out of the side of his mouth, Billy murmured, "I guess that's us." He steered the car along the dusty track toward the low house.

Grace coughed at the rising dust, pressing a hanky to her nose.

They pulled into the opening between two of the buildings, and Billy stopped the car. The silence was profound.

The dog woofed once, the sound cut off suddenly as if he'd been cuffed.

Two brown hens squawked and flapped away.

In the shadows sat a man, his chair tipped back against the wall. Grace swallowed hard. He looked like he hadn't shaved in days. A dark pipe hung from his mouth. The dog lay at his side.

"What ken I do fer you?" The words, spoken around the pipe, were barely distinguishable.

Billy remained in the car. Grace wondered if he had the same uneasy feeling she did. "I'm Billy Marshall. This is my wife. We moved into the old Martin place."

The man nodded without speaking, smoke puffing around his face.

"We heard you might have chickens to sell."

Billy's words fell into silence.

The man tipped his head toward one of the low buildings. "The missus is over there. Ya best be talking to her."

Billy got down and walked around to Grace's door. "You better come with me," he murmured to her, taking her hand as she stepped down beside him.

They marched across the yard. Grace felt the eyes of both man and hound on her back. It wasn't until they stepped into the indicated building that she could take a proper breath.

The building was some sort of workroom. Bunches of plants hung from the rafters; jars filled with an assortment of leaves lined the shelves. A wooden trestle table stood against one wall. On it lay more leaves and what appeared to be roots of a plant.

The room had a peculiar odor, not entirely unpleasant. Grace sniffed. "There's something familiar about that smell."

"Reminds me of the hospital," Billy muttered.

Grace sniffed again. "Maybe that's what it is. Do you see anyone?"

"No. Hello," he called, making Grace jump.

"Out here." The bodiless voice came from the door facing them, and they picked their way past the shelves and table and stepped back into the light.

A woman sat with a washtub between her knees, rubbing feathers from the lifeless body of a beheaded chicken. The smell half choked Grace, and she clutched Billy's hand.

Grace turned her gaze from the steaming wet feathers to the

woman at the tub. She had the blackest hair Grace had ever seen and eyes so dark there appeared to be no pupils;,eyes that stared straight through her.

"I'm Willow Welty. That no count man out there is my husband, Johns."

Her voice was low and deep, almost expressionless, even when she mentioned her husband.

"I'm sorry I can't be shaking your hand, but you can see I'm a mite busy right now."

Billy again introduced them and stated his request.

"Zeke, you come here now." The woman barely raised her voice, but a lanky youth Grace guessed to be thirteen or fourteen stepped from the shadows.

"This be my oldest, Ezekiel." She turned to the boy. "Where are your brothers and sisters?"

"Hiding." Zeke darted a look at Billy and Grace as if to indicate they were the reason for the others hiding.

"Get me a bucket of cold water and call the others."

Zeke nodded, grabbed a pail, and darted away.

"I'll be with ya in a minute." The woman returned to sliding her hand across the chicken, revealing pinkish skin beneath.

Grace vowed she would never eat chicken again.

Zeke reappeared with water, and Mrs. Welty plunged the chicken in the pail, washing her hands in the same water, drying them on her apron. She stood and faced Billy and Grace.

"I could spare you some youngish hens. These are the rest of my youn'uns." She beckoned over her shoulder, and a string of children stepped forward.

For the first time the woman smiled. "Mary and Baby."

A tall girl holding a dark-haired toddler nodded and smiled.

"My boys Daniel, Hosea, Jonah, Joel."

Stair steps, all younger than Mary, the children were as different as man and wife: one as dark as their mother; another with reddish hair like the father; another with freckles; and the youngest boy with light brown hair and a dark complexion. Grace thought he would grow into a handsome man.

Grace smiled at the children. "I'm pleased to meet you."

They seemed startled. She guessed it was her accent. "I'm from England. That's why I sound funny."

Daniel laughed first. "You sure do."

The others smiled shyly.

"It's right neighborly of you to come calling." Mrs. Welty shook feathers from her apron. "We'll have tea before we get down to business."

Mrs. Welty headed toward the house, indicating Billy and Grace should follow. The children trooped after them. Grace felt their subtle scrutiny.

Mr. Welty still puffed on his pipe, his chair still tipped back. Nothing on him had moved since they'd passed him earlier—nothing but his lips as he sucked on his pipe, blowing smoke through his nostrils.

"Mary, give Baby to yer father so's ya can help me."

The older girl dumped the baby on Mr. Welty's knee. He shifted the little one against him. The baby gave him a toothless grin. Mr. Welty winked at the child.

"Ya visit with Johns," Mrs. Welty said to Billy. "Ya come visit with me," she told Grace.

Startled by the order, Grace dropped Billy's hand and obeyed, wondering how the family all crowded into such a small area. A large plank table filled most of the kitchen. Through one door, a narrow room held space for nothing but the bed. Through a second door were two narrow beds and another door. The house was surprisingly clean and tidy.

"Set a spell." Mrs. Welty nodded toward the bench next to the table, and Grace sat. "Mary, set out some of them cookies you made."

The older lady studied Grace until Grace squirmed and looked away.

"Sorry, but I was thinking yer such a young thing. Not much older than my Mary and so far from home. How ya be doing?"

At the soft concern in her voice, Grace jerked her eyes upward. "I–I'm managing," she stammered, but her fears and uncertainties welled up. Tears flooded her eyes.

Mrs. Welty patted her shoulder. "There's no shame in a few tears." She waited until Grace took a deep breath. "It be hard at first—being on yer own."

Grace nodded.

Mary set a syrup pail of cookies on the table.

"Take some to the boys."

Mary dumped half the pail into her apron and hurried outside.

"If ya ever need a friend, ya give me a holler."

"Thank you."

"Now I'd better be making that tea before Johns starts to roar."

Grace smiled. She could detect no rancor in the woman's voice and wondered if her comments about her husband were simply her way of talking.

"There be much a woman has to learn."

Grace tried to laugh but it sounded strangled. "Mrs. Welty, I wasn't taught any of the things I need to know, so I suppose you could say I have more learning to do than most."

"Call me Willow. It's what I'm used to. And don't you be a-worrying about what you know or don't know. You'll catch on soon enough. Tea's ready. You want to fix up a cup for yer mister?"

Grace nodded, understanding the men were to take their tea outside together while the women remained inside. She didn't mind. Mr. Welty made her nervous.

After the men had been served their cups of tea and a handful of cookies, the two women sat across from each other at the table, Willow's dark eyes probing Grace. Finally, she nodded. "Ya'll do fine."

Grace couldn't understand why Willow's words made her feel better, but they did. "Do you mind if I ask you a question?"

The dark eyes never blinked. "Go right ahead."

"What were all those things in the building we came through?"

The shadow of a smile crossed her mouth. "My herbs. My people are healers. My mother, my grandmother, her mother, as far back as anyone can remember." Her smile was proud. "I have the gift."

Grace hoped her eyes didn't reveal her doubts.

"It's knowledge as much as gift," Willow continued.

"These are good," Grace said and took another bite of a molasses cookie. "Do you suppose I could learn to make some?"

"No reason why not. Mary, tell Grace what ya put in them."

Mary nodded. "Three spoons of lard, an equal amount of molasses, four eggs—"

"Wait. Do you have a piece of paper I could write it on?"

Mary rose and found a scrap of brown paper bag and handed it to her. "We got a pencil, Ma?"

Willow nodded. "Look on my dresser."

Mary came back with a stub of pencil hardly big enough to hold and recited the ingredients while Grace wrote them down. Grace wondered if the family could read or write but didn't want to ask.

"Now let's us go see about some hens." Willow led the way outside. "Get us a crate for some chickens," she told Zeke.

The baby slept on Mr. Welty's knee, and the youngest son, whom Grace guessed to be about three or four, played so close to the tipped-up legs of the chair, she wondered if it was safe.

Billy rose to go with them, but Mr. Welty didn't move. "I'll be letting Baby have her sleep."

" 'Sea and Dan'el, come give me a hand."

The two boys trooped after their mother.

Willow led them past the first dusty building. Chickens scurried after her. "No food right now, ya dumb things," she said, shoving them aside with her foot. "You boys catch up a dozen of those young pullets."

Daniel and Hosea—Grace couldn't remember which was

which—dashed after chickens. Birds squawked, running first one way, then another. The boys laughed as they dove after them, captured them, and stuffed them in the wire crate Zeke had brought.

Grace's laughter rang out. It was such a ludicrous sight, and it had been such a long time since she'd felt so light-hearted and silly. There was something about Willow's low gentle voice, her brood of children, even her husband that made Grace feel relaxed and sure of herself for the first time in many weeks. Willow was right. There was much to learn, but she'd catch on soon enough.

"That'll be sufficient," Willow said, as the crate grew crowded.

She led the way back between the crowded buildings, picked up a knife, tested it on her thumb, then bent over the pail. With a deft cut, she opened the bottom end of the chicken, shoved in her hand, and scooped out the entrails.

Grace knew her mouth had fallen open.

Willow scrubbed the carcass in the water, shook it, and held it out. "Ya might as well enjoy this. I got plenty more for us."

Grace shook her head. "No need for that." In truth she couldn't bear the thought of eating it.

"Thank you, Mrs. Welty," Billy said. "It will be a welcome change for us. We haven't been able to get much meat yet."

She nodded. "Figured as much. Didn't take you for a hunter."

Grace shuddered. She longed for a good joint of meat, but preferred to go to the butcher and select it oven ready.

Billy and Zeke carried the squawking, feathered cage to the car and tied it to the back.

For the first time, Mr. Welty dropped his chair to all fours, shifted the still sleeping child into the crook of his arm, and ambled to the car. He was a tall, loose-framed man. "See you folks have one of them newfangled automobiles."

Billy patted the car. "A good, solid Model T Ford. Couldn't ask for anything more practical. Much more sensible than a horse. No hay to put up. No need to clean out a stall. All ready to go at a moment's notice. Unlike having to harness a horse."

There was a gleam in Johns Welty's eyes. Grace suspected not having to feed a horse appealed strongly to him.

"Hard to learn to operate one of these things?"

"Not at all. Grace will be learning to drive this one."

Again, Grace felt a shiver of apprehension. She'd hoped he'd forgotten.

The whole family clustered around the car. The boys circled it, touching it here and there. Mary and Willow peered inside, then stepped back. Two cats meowed over and joined them, wrapping around Mary's ankles.

"How you fixed for cats?" Willow asked.

"Need a cat to keep the mice down," Johns agreed.

Grace shot Billy a look. Every night they heard mice scratching in the walls. She lived in dread of encountering one when she opened the cellar door.

Billy smiled. "We do have mice, and Grace is not at all fond of them."

"Mary, run and get the momma cat." She turned to Grace. "You take home this cat and soon there be no more mice."

Mary returned with a calico cat and two half-grown kittens.

Willow explained, "If you take her kittens as well, she won't be wanting to come back home."

It made sense, so Grace found herself sitting in the car with a cat and two kittens in her lap. The naked carcass of the chicken wrapped in brown paper rested between her feet.

"Them young hens will do fine by you. Let them forage for theyselves and feed them a bit of grain and yer vegetable scraps. Give them a day or two to settle, and then ye'll have eggs a-plenty."

The entire family watched as Billy gave the crank a turn or two; the engine coughed and started. He got behind the wheel, released the brake, and turned around slowly, having to wait while the family parted before him.

Grace waited until they were a distance from the house before she demanded, "What am I supposed to do with this?" She jerked her head toward the offending chicken.

"Cook it, I suppose. No doubt there are instructions in that book you have."

She shuddered. "I don't think I can."

"Don't be silly. Where do you think all those roast chickens you love so much come from?"

"The butcher shop."

He chuckled. "At one time they wore feathers and a beak."

"Yuk. I don't want to think about it."

"I hear rabbit is as good as chicken. I've been thinking maybe I'd shoot some. You could skin and clean one for supper some night. I think I'll do that."

She practically gagged.

"Then maybe you shouldn't look a gift chicken in the mouth."

She groaned. "Sometimes your jokes are horrible."

"I'm hurt."

Dust swirled around them. She waved it from her face before she answered. "I don't see how you could be. You intend them to be as horrible as they are."

He chuckled. "Poor Gracie. Just think, you'll have to put up with it the rest of your life."

She thought about that for awhile. The rest of her life to get used to Billy and his teasing and his carefree attitude. The rest of her life to persuade herself he loved her despite her inabilities. A whole lifetime to prove to him she was worthy of love.

He slanted a look at her, his brown eyes warm and merry. "Well, hey. I didn't think it was that bad."

"Sorry."

"Having to put up with me for the rest of your life?"

"Oh no." She laughed. "I was thinking it works both ways. You'll have to put up with me as well."

His smile deepened, sending warmth into his eyes. "Know

something, Gracie? I don't think it's going to be that hard."

He drove on. "In fact, I quite look forward to it."

"Me too," she murmured, pleased at his remark. She longed to hear his confession of love again, but she comforted herself that it was implied in his words.

five

At the sound of a wagon pulling into the yard, Grace set aside her book and hurried outside. Old Len from the livery barn and another man, a stranger to Grace, pulled to a halt in a swirl of dust.

Grace wiped the sweat from her brow. The sun beat down as hot as the fire in the stove. Today of all days, when she had decided to bake cookies from the receipt Willow had given her, had to be extra hot.

Billy stepped from the shadowed doorway of the barn, looking cool and content.

Grace envied him the coolness of the barn interior.

"Gotcha a customer," Old Len hollered. "His car broke down, and he's in a hurry. I told him you could go as fast as anything in that airplane of yours."

"Billy Marshall at your service, Sir. Where is it you're wanting to go?" Billy asked the passenger.

"Red Boushee." The men shook hands. "I'm on my way to an important meeting at the oil fields of Turner Valley. Got to get there as soon as possible."

"I can do that."

"How long before we can be on our way?" The man jumped down.

"How long will it take you to climb in?"

"My sort of man. I'm on my way." He strode toward the plane. "If you can get me there in time, you can name your price. This meeting is too important to miss."

"Wait a minute, will you be wanting a ride back?"

"If you can wait until I'm through, I will certainly want a ride back."

"How long will your meeting take?" Billy strode after the

man. "I'm only asking so I can let my wife know."

The man finally slowed down and turned around. "I'm sorry. I got in such a hurry, I forgot my manners." He turned to Grace. "Pleased to meet you, Mrs. Marshall. The meeting could go late. Would you mind if your husband is away overnight?"

Charmed by his sudden courtesy, Grace shook her head. "That's quite fine."

"Then let's be on our way."

Grace stood back as they prepared to leave.

Old Len sat in his wagon. "I ain't never seen one of these things take off."

Grace nodded and smiled. It was obvious he wasn't going to miss this opportunity.

A few minutes later the plane was airborne. Billy waved to Grace, then set a course to the southwest.

She stared after him for several minutes. Already she missed him and wondered how she'd face the darkness without him.

"I guess I best get back to town." Len's voice startled her. She'd forgotten he was still there. "You be wanting to go to town," he added, "I could give you a ride."

"Thank you. I'd like that if you can spare me a few minutes to collect my things."

"You go right ahead. I don't mind waiting."

She raced indoors. The last of the cookies were done, and she dumped them on a cooling rack and threw a clean towel over them. She hurried about, gathering up her library books to exchange for new ones, considering for a moment whether to return *Establishing a Pioneer Home*. In the end, she set it down again. She'd keep it a few more days.

Hurrying out to join Old Len, Grace was amazed at how quickly the drive into town took. He let her down in front of the library, and she hurried inside.

"Back already so soon, Dear?" Mrs. Paige beamed as she hurried from between the shelves. "You must be one of those closet readers."

"I'm sorry. I don't understand what you mean."

Mrs. Paige giggled behind her hand. "Of course you don't. It's a term I made up. When I was younger, I would crawl in behind the coats and hide so Mother wouldn't find a chore for me to do instead of wasting my time reading." She snorted. "Since then I've discovered people come up with lots of ways to hide their reading."

Grace began to grin.

"One girl said she stuffed her book under the cushions on the sofa so she could pull it out every chance she got, then hide it quick if anyone came in." Mrs. Paige chortled. "I've heard of hiding a book in your apron, behind a text book, even in a coffee canister."

Grace laughed. "Long trips to the loo. Hiding in a tree."

"Funny how we feel so guilty about such a wonderful pleasure."

"Isn't it?" But Grace half-suspected Billy would think she should be doing something more valuable with her time.

Mrs. Paige talked as Grace poked through the books. "How are you folk settling in?"

"We're settling in fine. My husband is away today. He flew a man out to Turner Valley."

"How exciting. Imagine being able to fly. I'll bet it's something."

"I wouldn't know. I've never been up."

"Really?"

"One of us has to have our feet on the ground."

The librarian laughed. "Well put."

"We met the Weltys and got some hens from Willow. Now we have our own eggs."

"That's best. How did you perceive the Welty family?"

Grace recognized the bid for gossip. She wanted none of it. "They were most helpful. Even gave us an oven-ready chicken. It was good."

"She's an industrious woman."

Grace turned away to hide a smile. Mrs. Paige's lips pursed

in such a way as to indicate Willow might be industrious, but as for her husband. . .

"The heat's been hurting the gardens and crops some," Mrs. Paige continued when Grace kept silent on the subject of the Weltys. "Your garden suffering?"

"I don't have one. At least not this year. It was too late when we got here."

"Of course it was. What was I thinking? I'm sure you'll be able to find produce somewhere. Perhaps some of the neighbors. Seems to me Mrs. Welty grows a lot of vegetables. Guess she'd have to, to feed that brood of hers."

"I suppose so."

"And I bet she grows some of those herbs she uses."

Interested, Grace asked, "Herbs?"

"Yes, herbs. She's a healer. An herbalist I guess you'd say." The librarian brightened, pleased at having found something Grace was interested in. "By all reports, she really does have the gift."

"Or the knowledge."

"Yes. Whatever. There are folks round here who swear by her methods."

"What about the doctor?"

"Doc Martin? I doubt he minds. He travels so many miles, he's probably glad to know there's someone here when he's away."

Grace carried the books she'd selected to the desk and waited for Mrs. Paige to check them out and carefully mark the due date on the card glued inside the back cover.

"It was so nice to see you again," she said, handing the books to Grace.

"I'll be back soon," Grace promised as she left, turning toward the post office. There were two letters for Billy—she recognized the names of his soldier buddies—as well as a letter from Billy's parents addressed to them both, and one from Irene. She slipped them in her pocket to read at home. With nothing else she wanted to do in town, she headed back.

At the crossroads she turned left. With the whole after-noon ahead of her, she decided she would visit Nellie.

Tom, bent over some piece of machinery, looked up and saw her as she drew close to the house. "Hello, there. We wondered how long before you'd get the time to come visit. Nellie's inside. Go ahead." He called out, "Nellie, Dear, you have company."

Nellie came to the door. "Grace. Come in. I'm so glad to see you. I've been wanting to show someone what I've been doing. How have you been?"

Grace laughed at her exuberant welcome. "I'm fine. How about you?"

Nellie rubbed her tummy. "Starting to feel a little big and awkward but otherwise healthy as a horse."

She led the way through the kitchen. "I'm almost ready for baby. See." She waved at the little items laid out on the sofa.

Grace stared. "You made all this?"

"Everything."

"It's lovely." She picked up a lacy white shawl. "This must have taken ages."

"Not that long. I started as soon as I knew I was going to have a baby. There are so many things to get ready." She touched the little nappies. "Do you think these will do?"

Grace picked one up and saw that Nellie had handstitched each hem. "I don't know anything about what babies need, but these look good enough for royalty."

Item by item, Nellie showed her what she'd done. "Four pairs of bootees. Two sweater sets. Little shirts." She held one up. "Isn't it tiny?"

Grace touched the garment. "I can't imagine something that small and yet completely human." She studied Nellie's glowing face. "Aren't you a little afraid?"

Nellie's smile was serene. "Of what? Birthing?"

Grace shook her head, looking away. "Of caring for a newborn baby," she murmured. "I don't think I've even held a brand-new baby."

Nellie laughed. "You'll catch on quick enough when it's your turn."

"I suppose so." Why did everyone assume she would automatically know what she needed to when the time was right? Somehow she didn't think being handed a tiny infant would provide her with a sudden wealth of knowledge.

"I'm sorry. I didn't mean to give you a pat answer." Nellie touched her hand. "Tell you what. I'll give you some lessons starting right now, and when my baby is born, I'll teach you what you need to know."

Grace blinked back a stinging in her eyes. "I would really like that," she whispered.

"First, you need to prepare for a baby." Nellie listed the many items needed. She stopped in the middle to explain how to care for soiled nappies, a bemused expression on her face as she pressed her hands to her tummy. "Put your hands here," she told Grace. "I want you to feel this."

When she saw Grace hesitate, she said it again. "You can feel the baby kicking."

Gingerly, Grace touched Nellie's swollen tummy.

Nellie laughed and pressed Grace's palm firmly to the roundness. "We won't break."

At first Grace felt only the firmness of the tummy, surprised at how hard and compact it felt. And then she felt an unmistakable thud against her palm and then another, and she laughed. "That's amazing."

"It's wonderful. Every time I feel it, I thank God for this precious gift."

Grace studied Nellie's serene expression. "I think I envy you."

"But why? You're married to your handsome flying ace. You're just beginning a new life together. And soon, no doubt, you'll have babies of your own."

There was so much Grace didn't know. "How did you know about the baby in the beginning?"

"Morning sickness was my first clue. And then the other things."

Grace laughed. "Maybe I'm going to have a baby then. Every morning when I get a whiff of that mouse smell, my stomach recoils in the most violent way." She almost gagged thinking about it. "At least it's better now that we got a cat and she's been catching mice by the bushel."

Nellie's eyes narrowed. "You're sure it's the mouse smell?"

"Yes." But she wasn't sure. How could she be? Her monthly cycle had always been so irregular.

"I've been thinking of you," Nellie continued.

"Good thoughts, I hope."

"Very good. I know you don't have a garden this year, so I've been wanting to give you some vegetables."

"That's not necessary."

"Of course it isn't, but I have more than enough."

"If you're sure?"

"I am very sure. Now come with me." She led the way to an immense garden.

"This isn't a garden." Grace gulped. "It's a farm."

Nellie laughed. "I like working here."

"Isn't it a little hard with—" Grace nodded at Nellie's swollen middle. "You know what?"

"It's getting harder as I get bigger, but Tom promised he'd help. Now how about some carrots?" She pulled some and put them in the basket she'd picked up as they left the house. She paused to scrub two clean on a corner of her apron. "Here, try one." She handed one to Grace and bit down on the other.

The carrot snapped between Grace's teeth. "Umm. These are delicious."

Nellie gave her carrots, potatoes she stole from under the plant, enough peas and beans for a couple of meals, and beets.

"This is wonderful. How can I ever thank you enough?"

"By coming to visit me often."

"That's a pleasure not a payment."

"It's all I want."

"Then I'll be over here so often you'll start locking the door when you see me come."

Nellie laughed and hugged her. "I don't think so. Now come to the house, and I'll make us tea."

As they sipped tea and ate sugar cookies, Nellie paused. "Will we see you in church on Sunday?"

"I expect so." They had both been raised to attend regularly.

"Are you a believer?"

"I'm not sure what you mean."

Nellie laughed. "I mean, are you a Christian? One who belongs to God's family?"

"Oh yes. I went to church school every Sunday back home. There was a sweet old lady who taught us what she called 'Lessons for the Highway to Heaven.' One of the first lessons told how sin had entered the world and how we were all sinners by birth and by choice. Then she said we had to take care of the sin problem before we could go to heaven, only we couldn't do it because we're sinners. Then she explained God had taken care of it. It was a gift we only had to accept. When she asked who wanted to accept that gift, I said I did."

"That's wonderful. God is my best friend. I couldn't imagine living without knowing Him. I talk to Him about everything: the baby, Tom, my garden, you—"

"Me?"

"Of course. Every day I ask God to bless your day and draw you closer to Him."

"You do?" Grace couldn't hide her amazement. "I don't remember anyone ever saying they prayed for me before."

Nellie laughed. "I'm sure people have; they just haven't told you."

"Perhaps." The idea was entirely too new to grasp.

"You'll like our little church," Nellie said, returning to her original subject. "Everyone is so friendly, and the pastor is a godly man who opens the Word to us every Sunday. He makes me hunger for more."

Grace nodded. "I'm looking forward to attending." And suddenly, listening to Nellie's excitement, she was.

It wasn't until hurrying home, burdened with books and produce, that Grace had a chance to reflect on Nellie's words. Was it possible to have God as one's friend? If only it were.

She ate four carrots on her walk home. It seemed she couldn't get enough of them and ate three more as she prepared a supper of eggs and salad for herself.

The evening stretched ahead, quiet and empty, echoing around her.

She chose one of her new books and curled up in the rocking chair. A snapping noise outside the window brought her to her feet, heart pounding. She crept to the side of the window and peeked out, vowing she'd hang curtains first thing in the morning. She watched and waited a moment but saw nothing but a swirl of leaves and tall scraggly weeds swaying in the breeze.

"Probably a seed pod on the weeds snapping," she assured herself, but before she sat down to read again, she pulled her chair into a corner away from the windows.

She couldn't concentrate. The house was suddenly full of mysterious sounds. Something creaked in the bedroom.

"It's only a board sighing," she muttered. Even her own voice seemed loud.

Scratching came from behind her, and she jerked to her feet. "A mouse." She knew what to do about the mice, and she hurried outside before she could ask herself if someone could be out there.

In the barn, she called, "Kitty, kitty."

The cat she'd brought from the Weltys jumped out of a manger, meowing.

"Bring your babies and come with me," Grace said, grabbing the two kittens from their straw nest.

The mother cat ran after her, meowing.

In the house, Grace put a blanket on the floor for the two kittens. The mother cat sniffed around, then waited at the cellar door.

"You go get them." Grace opened the door and let her down the stairs. "Now maybe I can settle down and read."

But a clatter downstairs brought her to her feet. She hurried to the doorway, screaming when the cat bounded up, a mouse crunched between its jaws, and dropped it on the blanket for the kittens. Growling, they pounced on the lifeless body.

A shudder raced down Grace's spine. Choking back a gag, she hurried back to the front room and her book.

Determined to ignore the sounds outside, closing her ears to the crunching coming from the kitchen, she read until the light faded. She knew she should go to bed, but the idea of crawling into bed alone in an empty house made her jaw quiver.

She sat in the chair, staring into the dusk.

The cat purred around her feet.

Grace reached down and rubbed the animal's back. "If you don't bring me any mice, you can sleep on my bed." She went to the kitchen. A tiny skull lay on the blanket. She flicked it away before she picked up the bundle of blanket and kittens and carried it to the bedroom. She settled them on the foot of the bed, then got undressed. The mother cat jumped up and lay down with the kittens. They nudged closer and began to nurse as Grace slipped under the covers. She closed her eyes, the gentle purring of the mother cat comforting.

Next morning, she returned the cats to the barn. "Thank you for helping me through the night."

The mother cat meowed as if she understood what her role had been.

After breakfast, Grace went to the end of the bedroom where boxes were stacked and opened one of them in which her mother-in-law had packed extra curtains and linens. Grace decided on lace curtains and heavy green brocade drapes. Most of the windows had rods over them, but she needed to fix the end of one rod before it would support the weight of the drapes.

She made a trip to Billy's workshop and found a hammer and nails. She bent the first nail, but the second she managed to drive into the wood, then threaded the rod through the curtains. The first window done, she stood back and surveyed the results.

The lace panel was a little skimpy when the drapes were pushed back, but the brocade material was heavy. "It will be almost impossible to see in after dark."

She did the other window, then wandered outside and pulled some of the weeds from the front of the house. Many were already going to seed, their bony branches dry and raspy. No wonder they rattled and snapped in the wind. She threw them into a pile, pausing to push her hair back from her face.

She had finished the length of the house when she heard a roar and glanced up to see Billy approaching.

Her shoulders relaxed. She wiped her hands on her apron and brushed her hair back. If only she had time to run to the house and tidy up, but already the airplane taxied toward the barn and rolled to a stop.

Mr. Boushee jumped down first, then Billy.

A lump rose in Grace's throat as she watched her husband glance toward the house. He pulled off his flying helmet. Sunlight caught in his shining dark hair. When he saw her watching, he grinned and waved.

Tears blurred Grace's vision. One day away, less than twenty-four hours, and she'd missed him so much. If Mr. Boushee hadn't been there, she would have run to Billy's arms and demanded a kiss or two. As it was, she had to content herself with walking sedately to his side and smiling up at him when he draped his arm around her shoulders.

"We're back safe and sound," he said.

"Your husband knows how to fly this thing," Mr. Boushee said. "Billy, thank you for making it possible to get to my meeting in time." He unfolded a handful of bills and handed Billy forty dollars.

"Whoa. That's way too much."

Mr. Boushee shook his head. "It was worth every penny. Besides, I was going to ask you to give me a ride to town." He nodded toward the Model T. "I see you like to drive as well."

"I prefer machines to animals." Billy chuckled.

The other man laughed.

"I won't be long," Billy murmured to Grace before he released her to hurry to the car. "Anything you need in town?" he asked as he stood ready to turn the crank.

"No, I was there yesterday."

He nodded and gave the crank a turn. The engine coughed to life.

Grace waved as they drove from the yard, then hurried inside to think about what to make for dinner.

In the end she settled for using the last bottle of meat she had purchased from Mr. Tunney and cooking up some of the vegetables Nellie had given her. Nellie had offered to provide them with meat from her store of canned beef. "You can pay me back when you butcher in the fall." She'd gone on to explain how a butchering ring worked. "Neighbors get together and share a beef. That way no one has a whole animal to deal with at once. Everyone takes turns providing the animal to butcher."

"But we don't have any animals."

Nellie nodded. "You could have one on your pasture if you wanted. Or you could simply buy one ready to butcher when it's your turn."

It made sense to Grace. She'd wanted to bring some meat home right away, but it was too heavy to carry. She'd mention it to Billy as soon as he got home. Maybe he'd take the auto over.

She brought up the subject over dinner.

"We'll go this afternoon. I can kill two birds with one stone and teach you to drive at the same time."

Grace dropped her fork with a clang. "I hoped you would forget about me driving."

Billy stared at her. "Of course I won't. It makes perfect sense."

She grimaced. "Trying to teach me to handle something that size when I can barely manage to produce a meal doesn't make one bit of sense."

He grabbed her hand. "Grace, will you stop putting yourself

down all the time? You are far more capable than you let your-self think. This—" he nodded at his plate—"is a very decent meal. In fact, it's excellent. You amaze me with how quickly you catch on." He paused, but she only stared at him. "I have no doubt you can drive a car, run a house, or anything else you put your mind to—probably even fly an airplane."

She gasped. "Fly an airplane? I couldn't."

He grinned. "Well, maybe not. I probably wouldn't let you practice on *Gracie Two*, but you know what I mean."

She only shook her head.

He sighed. "Gracie, why must you believe that all you have going for you is your looks?" He grinned. "Not that I have anything against having a beautiful wife, but you are so much more, and you can't see it."

She looked away, too confused to answer.

He waited a heartbeat, then pushed back. "Come on. I'll help you clean up, and then we'll get on with driving lessons." He stacked the dishes and carried them to the washing-up stand.

Sighing deeply, she put away the food, then washed while he dried. But she could not relax, knowing what was to follow.

They stood in front of the car.

"I think the first thing you need to know is how handy it will be to be able to drive. You can visit Nellie, run over and see the Weltys, or see whoever else you want to visit in a matter of minutes. You'll soon get used to going twenty miles an hour. Just think of all the time that will save you."

She nodded, unconvinced.

"You can go to town and get as many supplies and books as you like and not have to worry about trundling home under the weight."

At the mention of books, she shot him an apprehensive look, but his attention was on the auto.

"Now have you been paying attention?"

"I always pay attention." She had no idea what he meant but determined to make a good showing, prepared to prove her worth.

"Then what's the first thing you do?"

"Turn the crank." She stepped to the handle and, throwing her weight into it, gave the crank a spin.

"Be careful, it has a—"

She felt the crank connect with whatever it did inside the engine, then it kicked back with a force that almost sent her headfirst into the hood. She stepped back and gaped at the auto.

"I was going to say, be careful, it has a kick when it connects." He almost choked as he tried to suppress his amusement.

Grace gave him a slanted look. "I noticed."

His eyes danced with laughter. "Try again. This time, prepare for the kick."

She gritted her teeth, tightened her fists around the crank, and again threw her weight into it, this time refusing to let the heavy thrust throw her. She was rewarded with a sputter, then the engine roared to life. She stepped back and grinned at Billy. "Nothing to it." She dusted her hands together.

Billy laughed. "Told you. Come on, get behind the steering wheel."

She sobered. Starting the engine was only the beginning. Her jaw felt brittle as she climbed up behind the wheel. Suddenly, the ground looked very far away; the bonnet of the auto very long. How would she control this monster?

"Grace, pay attention. The pedals are very important. Try them out and know what each is for. Right for braking; left for neutral and the two forward gears; the middle is for backing up."

She repeated his words and tried her feet on the pedals.

"Now this—" he showed her the handle beneath the steering wheel—"is the throttle. It controls how fast you go. This is the hand brake and clutch." He waited while she repeated every word. "Now, push the brake ahead and push on the left pedal."

She did as he said, her breath caught in her chest. The car jerked forward. She screamed. "What do I do?"

Grinning widely, he sat back, his arms crossed over his chest. "Take the steering wheel and head down the road."

She wrinkled her nose. It was obvious he wasn't going to be

any help except to fling about orders, so she grabbed the wheel with both hands, her knuckles white against the black steering wheel. Biting her lip, she felt the power beneath her palms.

The car veered toward the grass on the right side.

She darted a panicked look at Billy, but he leaned back, grinning.

She turned the wheel to right the course and it headed for the left side. Slowly she brought the steering wheel back to center. The car stayed in the middle of the trail.

She let her breath out in a gush and began to giggle. "I did it. I did it. Oh no, I have to turn. Billy, help me."

"Just turn the wheel whatever direction you want to go."

Her heart racing, she cranked right. The car ambled around the corner and headed for the ditch. She wheeled toward the left. *Slowly, slowly*, she reminded herself, until she stayed in the center.

She sighed. "Am I doing all right?"

"More than all right. You're doing very well."

She beamed at him, bouncing up and down on the seat.

"Now maybe you should pull back on the throttle. Remember where it is?"

"Here?" She touched the lever.

"That's right. Pull back just a little."

She did as he said, gasping back a scream when the automobile jerked forward, rattling along at a frightful pace. "Too fast, too fast," she yelled.

Billy laughed. "Just watch where you're going."

She blinked hard, her hands clenching the steering wheel. After a few minutes, the speed seemed less intimidating.

"By the way, where are we going?" Billy asked.

She didn't take her eyes from the road. "Can we go to the Deanses?"

"Good idea. Do you want to practice stopping before we get there?"

She'd only begun to breath easy, and now her lungs tightened up again. "Stop. How do I stop?"

"Pull back the throttle. That's the one beneath the steering wheel."

She did as he said.

"Now push the left pedal twice. And pull on the hand brake."

She did as he said, and they jerked to a stop.

"Wasn't that fun?"

"It was scary." A laugh tickled the back of her throat and escaped. Suddenly, for no apparent reason, it seemed very funny, and she laughed so hard, tears ran down her cheeks.

"See, I told you it would be fun. Almost as much fun as flying."

"Never."

"Someday. Now do you want to go see Nellie or not?"

She sat up straight. "Let's go."

"First the—"

"I can do it." Steadying herself with a deep breath, she repeated the steps he had told her and headed down the road toward the Deanses.

six

Billy pulled the car in beside the other autos and buggies in front of the church.

Grace waited for him to come around and help her down, smoothing her gloves and removing the kerchief she'd tied around her hat to keep the dust off. She wiped her face with her handkerchief, then took Billy's hand and stepped down. "You know, I like going to church."

"You do?" Billy stopped to give her a startled look.

"You don't have to look so surprised."

"I'm sorry, but I can't help thinking how annoyed you were back in Britain that your father made you go."

She wrinkled her nose. " 'It won't do you any harm, and it might do you some good,' " she droned in imitation of her father. "Honestly, I would have sooner stayed home any day and read a good book. But this church is different."

"You've made that conclusion after what—four weeks?"

"I knew it was different from the beginning."

Billy pulled her hand through his arm and led her toward the church steps. "I think you just welcome the chance to get all dressed up."

Grace patted her hat, then swirled her skirt a little as she walked. "It's a fine dress and bonnet, isn't it?" She'd bought them both at Church's store in town.

Billy grinned down at her. "It certainly looks fine on you."

"Thank you, Billy. I confess I like to wear my nice things, but that isn't why I like church. Nor is it because I get to see Nellie. I could simply drive over and spend the hour visiting if that were the case."

"True enough." He paused at the bottom of the steps. "Perhaps it helps that you aren't being forced to go."

73

"That makes me sound petty and rebellious. No, it's because what the Reverend Albright says makes sense. He makes me want to listen."

"I am impressed. But I agree. He is a good speaker."

They stepped inside, ending the conversation, but Grace promised herself they'd finish it later. She didn't mean only that the Reverend Albright was a good speaker; she meant his words tugged at something inside her.

They edged in beside Tom and Nellie. Nellie squeezed Grace's hand. "I'm glad to see you," she whispered.

Grace leaned close so no one else would hear her. "How are you feeling?"

Nellie wrinkled her nose. "Big and awkward." She rubbed the side of her stomach.

The organist began to pump out hymns, and the Reverend Albright rose to his place behind the pulpit.

Nellie had a full-throated singing voice that made Grace enjoy singing the hymns. Then Rev. Albright opened his Bible and leaned over the pulpit. "What a friend we have in Jesus."

From his first word, Grace listened intently. He made it sound so possible, so wonderful. But it was so different from her experience, she wondered how he could be right.

After the service, Nellie turned to her. "I prepared a cold lunch. We were hoping you'd share it with us in the park."

Grace turned to Billy.

"Sounds like fun."

The four of them were soon seated on blankets in the park. Grace helped Nellie put out the food. As they ate, she glanced around the park. Others were also enjoying a Sunday picnic.

"There's Old Len. He's with someone."

"That's his sister, Maude," Nellie said. "They live together in that little cottage beside the livery barn." She nodded toward others, pointing out who they were and where they lived.

The meal over, Grace jumped up to put things away. "You sit right there," she told Nellie.

Nellie sank back. "Thank you, Grace. I don't mind if I do. I've been so tired all week."

Tom pulled her down to lay her head in his lap. "Of course, she won't listen to me when I tell her to take it easy."

"I want to get everything done before the baby comes."

"You don't have to can enough stuff for five families," Tom scolded.

Grace glanced at Billy, stretched out on the blanket, his eyes closed, his chest gently rising and falling. She was almost certain he had fallen asleep. She sat close to him, longing to have him lay his head in her lap so she could caress his forehead and stroke his hair, but she didn't want to waken him. Instead, she turned toward Nellie. "Couldn't I help you with the garden and canning? You could teach me how to do it at the same time."

Tom's eyes lighted with gratitude.

Nellie spoke without opening her eyes. "I would like to teach you. And you could help me by taking some of the excess off my hands."

Monday morning, Grace did the laundry, but as soon as she cleaned up after breakfast the next day, she drove over to Nellie's where Nellie already had a large tub of beans picked.

They sat together, tipping and tailing beans, washing and boiling them, packing them into jars, then slipping them into the hot water bath.

Grace wiped the perspiration from her brow. "This is hot, hard work. No wonder you've been tired. Exactly how many jars have you done up already?"

"I've lost track, but somewhere around one hundred twenty, I think."

"What on earth will you do with all that?"

Nellie gave her gentle, unruffled smile. "Eat it, I suppose. Oh, I know it's more than Tom and I will eat in a winter, but with a child coming and all. . ." She lifted one shoulder. "I guess it's my mother's fault. She always said she liked to have a year ahead in case the garden failed. Besides, I have enough to share with you."

Feeling guilty that she might be the cause of Nellie having too much to do, Grace returned to preparing beans. "It's an awful lot of work."

"I know, but it's so nice to go down to the cellar in the middle of winter and see those jars of food."

"I suppose it's nice to know you don't have to worry about going hungry."

For a moment they worked in silence, then Grace turned the conversation to another topic. "What did you think of the Reverend Albright's sermon?"

Nellie's whole face lit up with her smile. "I thought it was wonderful and so true. Just the reminder I needed."

"But he made it sound like God is as close as you are to me."

Nellie nodded. "He is. He's a friend that sticks closer than a brother."

"I never had a brother; only my sister, Irene, who was really more like a mother than a sister. She accompanied me to Canada."

"Where is she now?"

Grace smiled. "She's in Alberta. She married Billy's cousin, a widower with two little boys."

"Didn't you have a close friend?"

"Addie King. She lived next door. Her parents let her have all sorts of freedom I wasn't allowed. So when we got together, we did things forbidden for me."

Nellie's hands were still for the first time all morning. "What sort of things?"

"Addie loved to climb trees." Grace laughed. "When Father caught me in the branches of the oak, I thought he would have a fit he was so upset. I was banned from playing with Addie for two weeks, and then we were under strict supervision of Irene."

"But why should he object so strongly?"

Grace shrugged and made a little face. "I guess I almost died as a baby and didn't thrive for a long time. I think they got used to protecting me."

"I don't understand then how you met Billy."

"It was forbidden for me to go near the hospital, but I disobeyed Father. It was so boring at home. Addie had long since moved to London; Irene and Father were both off at jobs. I was expected to sit at home and amuse myself quietly." She frowned, remembering the boredom. "I'm so glad Billy took me away from that stifling atmosphere. I was terrified at first about coming out to Alberta, but I like it, and it isn't at all forbidding."

"You're a plucky young lady."

Grace snorted. "I'm a fearful young woman, ill equipped to face the responsibilities of a wife. Thankfully, Billy is patient."

"Guess it helps that he's madly in love with you."

Eyes wide, Grace stared at Nellie.

Nellie blinked. "Why surely you know that?"

Grace could do no more than shake her head, tears choking her throat.

"Oh, Grace. How can you miss what's as plain as the nose on your face? Billy almost falls over his feet, he's so stuck on you."

Grace busied herself snipping beans while she steadied her thoughts. "I love him so much it frightens me."

For a moment, Nellie didn't reply, then in her gentle voice she said, "Love should never make you afraid."

Grace jerked her head up. "You're right. It shouldn't." She slumped forward. "But sometimes it does."

"But love is God's greatest gift. Not only does He love us, but He put in each of us the capacity to love and be loved."

"You sound like Rev. Albright."

Nellie laughed. "That's the nicest compliment I've had in a long time." She grew serious again. "If you mean because he said God's love makes it possible to be friends with Him, then it's because I agree with him."

"I guess that's the part I don't understand: How can we dare to call God a friend? It sounds irreverent to me."

"I suppose it would be irreverent if God didn't extend the invitation. Jesus said He called us friends, not servants.

Having said He wishes us to be friends, we have only to accept His offer."

"I see what you're saying," Grace murmured. But still she couldn't accept it. It didn't feel right to say a holy, almighty, powerful God could be your friend.

Nellie moaned softly, pressing her hand against her stomach. Grace sprang to her side. "Is something wrong?"

"No. Baby is getting a little crowded, that's all."

"I can handle these beans on my own until the next lot is due to go in the canner. You go lie down and rest awhile."

Nellie gave her a grateful look. "You sure you don't mind?"

"Of course I don't." She made shooing motions. "Go now."

"Thank you."

❧

"I'm going barnstorming," Billy said a few days later.

"What does that mean?"

"It means flying to every little town we can find and offering rides for two dollars. And if we get lucky enough to find a few fairs, we might persuade the town to pay fifty dollars to see some stunt flying."

Grace finally turned from scrubbing a pot she'd burned gravy in. Alarm shot through her veins, making her voice sharp. "Every town? Stunt flying? You said you wouldn't be doing any of that. You promised me."

Billy nodded, his expression regretful. "I know what I said and I meant it, but in the last month we've only had one man wanting to be taken to Banff and a trip to Turner Valley to deliver a package. If I don't do something, we'll go hungry this winter."

Grace choked back the sour panic rising in her throat. "I thought we had lots of money."

"We bought a car and an airplane. There's rent on this place. There's food and gasoline." He shrugged. "We had enough to get started." His voice dropped to a mumble. "I thought business would be better than it is."

Grace dropped to a chair.

He looked down at the floor. Suddenly, he brightened. "You've seen how interested people are in flying. I hear there's good money in barnstorming and doing fairs."

Still Grace said nothing.

"I figure we start down the highway, stopping at every little town, taking in every fair we can find. It's that time of year. We could make enough to last us the winter."

Only one word interested her. "We?"

"I'll fly *Gracie Two*, and you'll come along in the car. That way I have a way of getting around when I'm on the ground."

Grace stared at him, her mind whirling with a mixture of apprehension and excitement. Finally, she said, "I see."

"Makes perfect sense."

"Of course." Her thoughts were still too fragmented to know what she thought.

"We'll camp out to save money. It will be like our first night together here. That was fun, wasn't it?"

Her insides turned to butter. "It was. So what do we have to do to get ready? When are we leaving?"

Billy laughed. "I knew you'd be practical about this." He slapped his palms together. "Let's get organized." He began to list what they would need—bedding, a tarp for protection, food, dishes—

Grace threw up her hands. "It sounds like we're leaving immediately."

Billy laughed. "Let's wait until morning."

Dusk fell around them before they had everything packed in boxes and secured to the car.

"That's the works. Just one more thing." He gave Grace a narrow-eyed look.

She glanced down at her dress, now dusty and soiled despite the apron covering much of it. "What?"

"You know how dusty it will be in the car."

She nodded.

"I think you need to think about something more practical than fancy flowered dresses and useless women's shoes."

Her look was steady, suspicious. "What are you suggesting?"

"Come with me. I'll show you." He led her to the barn and pulled from a shelf a rolled-up bundle. "Here, try these." He flipped the bundle open. It contained a small flight suit, goggles, and a leather helmet. He reached up again and brought down a pair of leather boots.

Grace looked at them carefully. Everything was new and exactly the right size for her. "I see this whole idea is spur of the moment."

He laughed. "Yup. It just crossed my mind a few minutes ago."

"And you happened to have everything the right size just lying around."

He looked innocent. "Can't imagine what prompted me to buy them last time I was in Edmonton. Isn't life amazing?"

She giggled. "Not half as amazing as you."

It was his turn to look suspicious. "You mean that as a compliment, right?"

Tossing her head, she turned her back, heading toward the door. "What else?"

He hurried to her side. "You going to try them on now?"

She cast him a slanted look, seeing the eager light in his eyes. "If you'd like."

He nodded, his eyes ablaze.

He waited while she went in to remove her dress, stockings, and shoes and slip into the coveralls. She found a pair of Billy's socks, then pulled on the boots, surprised at how light and comfortable they were. Before she returned to Billy, she stood in front of the mirror, examining the effect.

The flight suit was form fitting. She blushed to see how it revealed her curves and narrow waist. Yet it sat easy on her shoulders. She knew it would protect her from the dust far better than her own clothes did. She bundled her long hair to the top of her head and tried to put on the helmet, but she had too much hair. Leaving the tight hat perched atop her head, she stepped outside for Billy to see.

He let out a long, low whistle, then circled her, studying

her figure in such a way as to make her cheeks grow hot.

"You're making me nervous."

"I'm only admiring the beautiful woman I married." He stood in front of her, pressing his finger to his chin, appearing to be in deep concentration. His gaze slid slowly up and down her figure, coming to rest at last on her face. "You know, you've grown more beautiful since we came west." He leaned closer, studying her face. "It's in your expression." His brows drew together. "You've lost that frightened little-girl look." He trailed warm fingers down her cheek, coming to rest on her chin. "You have become a beautiful, confident woman."

She giggled. "Not very womanly in this outfit."

His eyes twinkled. "Far more womanly than you can imagine." He bent and kissed her. "Now I think we need to do something about your hair."

"My hair?" Her hands automatically touched it.

"It will never fit into a helmet, and unless it does, you'll have to contend with the dust every day." He tilted his head from side to side. "How would you like one of those new, shorter styles?"

She'd seen pictures of young women with their hair shingled or cut into a boyish mop. It didn't seem quite right, yet, as Billy said, it would be far more practical. "Have you ever seen a woman with short hair?"

"Lots of them. You'd look really swell with your blond curls."

His admiration made her forget her own reservations. "I don't have time to get it cut."

"We can do it tonight."

"That 'we' business again. I'm supposing you propose to cut it for me?"

His eyes glistened. "I could. It doesn't look so hard."

"Billy, nothing looks hard to you."

"Am I ever wrong?"

"I suppose not. At least, not so far."

"Come on. Take a chance."

She gave in. "I guess it does make sense. But somehow I

fear I will regret letting you do this."

He cut her locks, letting them fall around her feet, then stood back and surveyed his work with a satisfied grin. "It looks good to me."

"Let me see." She rushed to the mirror. Her hair hung to her ears in loose curls. Billy had managed to shape it so it clung to her cheeks and forehead. Grace gasped. "I can't believe that's me."

"Didn't know you were so pretty, did you?"

She didn't answer, simply stared at this exotic stranger. Finally she turned away. "I can't get used to it." She shook her head. "I feel so light." Yet secretly, the cut pleased her. All her life she'd struggled with her heavy, curly hair. Irene had complained about the hours it took to wash and dry it and do it up in plaits or more grown-up styles. The idea of cutting it had never entered Grace's mind, and she was quite certain both Irene and Father would have had a fit if she'd suggested it. But it was the perfect answer. She shook her head again. "I think I like it."

"I knew you would. Aren't I always right?"

She giggled. "As if you would admit it if you weren't."

He pretended to be offended. "Of course I would. If I were." He pulled her close. "I like it too. Now I can feel it any time I want without worrying about you having to spend hours repairing the damage." As if to prove his point, he plunged his fingers through her curls, rubbing her scalp, sending pleasure through her veins.

❧

Billy stretched out on the ground beside the car. They had set up camp between the car and the airplane, a tarp stretched between the two.

Grace bent over the fire, stirring a pot of stew and checking the biscuits in the Dutch oven.

"It was another good day." Billy's voice was muffled.

"How many did you take up? I lost track after fifteen."

"This was the best day yet. I took up twenty. And one of them was from Rose Creek, the next big town on this line.

We talked about me doing a show there, and he said if I showed up Friday afternoon, they would feature me in the evening entertainment."

Grace paused. So far there had been no stunt flying, and she hoped it would remain that way. "It looks as if the weather will hold."

"Sure was hot today. How did you manage down here?"

She knew he meant on the ground. "I stayed in the shade."

They had been on the road almost two weeks and settled into an easy routine. Every morning, Billy got Grace to spin the prop, then took off in the airplane following the railway tracks and a maze of roads. At each town, Billy chose a level field nearby and landed *Gracie Two*. By the time Grace caught up, there were usually several people clustered around. Billy promised rides at two dollars each. Sometimes there were enough customers to start immediately. Other times, he drove into town and marched up and down the streets, telling everyone of his offer.

Every night they camped beside the airplane.

"Supper's ready." She handed him a plate of stew and some biscuits.

He sat up and dug into the food eagerly. "You sure are turning into a good cook." He waved a biscuit at her. "Not that I ever doubted you would. You can do anything you put your mind to."

"I like cooking outdoors. Guess I don't feel like I have to live up to anyone's expectations out here."

He gave her a quizzical look. "And whose expectations do you think you have to live up to at home? Certainly not mine. I think you do a fine job."

She shrugged. "It seems I should be able to do things better than I do."

"Grace, sometimes you are so blind. You do things perfectly well." He fell silent again as he cleaned his plate. "By the way, speaking of putting your mind to something, don't you think it's about time you came up with me in *Gracie*

Two? I could take you first thing tomorrow morning."

She shook her head. "I don't think so. I'm content to keep my feet on the ground. You can be the flier in the family."

He grabbed her about the shoulders and pulled her down on top of him. "Sometimes I think you don't trust me."

She rubbed noses with him. "You, I trust. But that bucket of bolts you fly—"

"Bucket of bolts!" He pushed her back. "After all the time I pour into *Gracie Two*, keeping her in top-notch condition, you dare call her a bucket of bolts?" He shook his head. "You'll pay for that." He threw her on her back and pinned her arms at her side before he plucked a feathery head of grass and tickled her face.

"Billy," she squealed, squirming in a vain attempt to escape his grasp. "Stop." She giggled, turning her head from side to side, trying to avoid him.

"Not until you say you're sorry."

"I'm sorry. I'm sorry."

He released her, and she squirmed out of reach. "I'm sorry your airplane is a bucket of bolts." She was running before he got to his feet. She made it fifty yards before he caught her and tackled her to the ground.

"This time, no mercy," he vowed. She kissed him, muffling his threats. When he slackened his hold on her arms, she started to giggle.

"What's so funny?" he muttered against her lips.

"I think I've discovered the best defense against tickling."

"Feel free to use it any time you like." He silenced her with another kiss.

Later, she lay in the crook of his arms, staring into the starlit sky. "I wish it could always be like this."

"Like what?"

"The two of us on our own with no responsibilities."

He jerked up on his elbow. "No responsibilities? Girl, you haven't been paying attention. There's both machines to keep running. Camp to set up every day. Meals to cook. Washing up, laundry. Everything there is at home as well as the customers to take care of. And you, I might add, are a real asset in lining up the schedule."

"It's not the same. Out here it's like pretend. No one expects things to be perfect, so it doesn't matter."

He flung himself over on his back. "Grace, my dear, you have a real problem with what you think people expect from you. How many times do I have to tell you no one expects you to be perfect? I'm quite content with you the way you are except for this haunting idea that someone is waiting to shoot you down." He turned to watch her. "I haven't a clue who you think that person would be. You know it's not me. It's certainly not Nellie. She's been nothing but supportive. Who does that leave? Only you." He paused, letting her digest his words. His voice softer, he continued. "I know your father and Irene treated you like you were a fragile bit of china, but I don't see that as reason for this fear of yours. What is it that's plaguing you, Gracie?"

She rolled her head side to side, staring miserably into the darkness. "I don't know. I only know it seems I can never be quite good enough." She waved away his protest. "I know what you say, but it doesn't still the accusations in my own mind."

Billy made a sound of exasperation. "Someday you are going to have to learn to trust and believe me."

"I know," she whispered. "But maybe it's more than that." She spoke the words so low she wondered if he heard.

seven

After a minute, Billy asked very quietly, "And what would that be? Is there something you haven't told me?"

"Oh no, nothing that should upset you. It's only. . ." How could she put into words what was nothing more than vague restless uncertainties? "I don't know. Maybe I'm being childish. But sometimes. . ." Her words trailed off.

"Sometimes what?" Billy's voice was low and insistent.

She threw her hands up. "Sometimes I feel like there's a vast emptiness inside me. And I don't know how to fill it." There she'd said it, but the words sounded hollow and silly in her ears.

Billy remained silent so long, she thought he had decided to ignore her, until he said in a low, deep voice, "Sometimes I feel empty too. But I found it goes away if I go do something I enjoy."

She stared into the darkness. Doing things only made her feel worse. Sure she would ignore the feeling, but the only time she really felt better was in church. "Remember when Rev. Albright talked about being friends with God?"

"Vaguely."

"Maybe that's what I need."

Again, her words met a long silence. Then Billy sighed. "If it works for you, then go for it."

"But that's it, don't you see? I don't know if it would work for me, and besides, I don't even know what 'it' is."

"Let me see if I can remember what he said. I know he talked about how God made a way for us to be right with Him."

"Yes, yes. Salvation through faith in Jesus. I know that. But there's more. I know there is. Nellie talks like there is." She rose on her elbow and pressed her palm to Billy's chest as if trying to force the answers she needed from him. "But what is that something more?"

He covered her hands with his. "Let me think. Hmm. Didn't the reverend say something about forgiveness being a part of it? That part of it is peace with God, and another part of it was the peace of God."

She sank back on the blanket. "I guess I'll never have that part of it."

"Why not?"

"I don't know. It just doesn't seem possible."

"Forget it for now. I'm sure the answer will come sooner or later. Right now I need some sleep, and so do you." He pulled her close. "Close those big blue eyes and settle down."

She snuggled close, not expecting sleep to come, but it claimed her immediately.

ta

Billy waited in the laneway as Grace drove into the yard.

"Home, sweet home," he said as she stopped the engine of the car and sat waiting for the cloud of dust to pass before she pulled the leather helmet from her head and shook her curls free.

"I don't know if I'm sorry or glad it's over," she said. "Seems more like we're saying good-bye than hello."

Billy, understanding that she meant it was hard to put the past month behind her, nodded. "The summer season is over. We've been across most of the southern part of the province and. . ." He shook his pockets. "We got enough money to last us a few more months. It's time we settled down."

She wanted to ask why. "Settling down sounds so— "

"Responsible?"

She laughed. "Do I sound like I'm trying to avoid accepting responsibility?"

He pulled her into his arms. "Not really. You've grown up a lot these past few months." He grinned down at her. "Wouldn't your father be surprised to see how much you've changed?" His expression sobered. "What do you tell him in the letters you send?"

"Mostly I tell him how I'm such a good cook, how we traveled across the province on 'business,' and what the country is like." She shook her head. "He'd never believe I'm capable of driving a car and handling the appointments and cooking out of doors." She laughed. "I can hardly believe it myself."

"You're a fine worker, Gracie One."

She laughed. "At least I'm still number one, though sometimes I wonder."

He kissed her nose. "Never wonder. You'll always be number one."

Tears choked at her throat at the tenderness in his voice.

"It's too bad you don't make friends with *Gracie Two* though." He leaned back to look in her face. "Now that would be a perfect ending to our travels."

"What?"

"Let me take you flying."

She wanted to say no. How many times had her heart caught in her throat as she watched him take others flying and heard the cough in the engine? She'd almost died of fright when the engine stalled as he turned loops at the show at Rose Creek. But he looked so eager. How could she refuse him? Finally, she nodded.

"Whoopee!" he yelled.

"Spoken like a true Albertan." She'd heard the cry repeated time and again as they crisscrossed the province.

"You won't regret this. I promise you. There is nothing like the thrill of looking down. It gives you a different perspective on everything."

"Just get me down safely," she muttered, following him to the airplane. He boosted her up so she could crawl into the forward seat, then scrambled into the back one.

A few minutes later they were airborne. Grace looked down on the house and yard, amazed at how neat they looked from the air. The air rushed past her face. She closed her eyes and breathed deeply. A rush of joy swept over her at the sense of freedom, and she laughed. She turned to face Billy. He grinned widely, then pointed downward.

Nellie and Tom stood beside their house, faces upturned. Grace waved madly. She could see their wide grins.

Billy turned their course toward town. They swept over it twice as Grace watched, fascinated at the activity below them. Billy was right. Life held a whole different perspective from up here.

He tapped her shoulder, and she turned to look back at him. He pointed to the south. "The river," he mouthed.

She nodded, and they skimmed toward the dark green line of trees that marked Red Deer River. Soon they looked down on thick treetops and flashing water. *This must be what peace feels like,* she thought. *A rush of air that cleanses one's thoughts; a distance that gives perspective; and a view that allows one to see far beyond the tiny spot of earth where one's feet are planted.* When Billy turned the plane homeward, she sighed, wishing they could go on forever.

The engine coughed. Grace stiffened, turning to watch Billy. He pulled at something in the cockpit, then gave her a reassuring grin and a thumb's-up sign. She turned back to watching the scenery speed by. Again the engine stuttered. She forced herself to relax. She'd heard the same sound a dozen times while standing on the ground. Billy had always landed safely. But when the engine coughed again and almost died, she gripped the frame of the airplane so hard her palms hurt.

The engine coughed again and died, the sudden quiet so intense she could hear every heartbeat thundering in her chest. They hung in space.

She turned to Billy. "What's the matter?" Her shouted words seemed obscenely loud.

Billy didn't look up from his concentration on the controls. "Don't worry. I'll get it going again."

But they were falling. The air rushed past her. She moaned. "I knew I shouldn't fly," she muttered.

"Duck down into the cargo space."

She heard his words; she knew what each meant; but she couldn't connect to them. She sat frozen, her hands locked in place.

"Grace." Billy's voice rang through her fear. "I'm going to bring her in, but it will be a little rough. I need you to crawl into that space at your feet."

She nodded. But still she couldn't make herself move.

Billy leaned forward to push on her head, but she could no more let go of her death grip than she could fly. She moaned. Wrong choice of words.

A squeal snaked through Grace's clenched teeth as the ground raced up to meet them. They touched down with a thud that jerked through her arms and bolted into her shoulder joints. Something snapped with the loud, angry sound of metal crumpling. The airplane spun to the left, throwing Grace against the metal frame. Searing pain ripped through her side. Agony made her loosen her grip, and she clutched at her side. A tree snapped before the plowing nose. The severed branch shot toward Grace.

≈

Grace ached all over. Cautiously, she opened her eyes, expecting to be in the airplane. Her eyes widened at the sight of her own bedroom.

Billy appeared in her line of vision. "Thank God you're awake. Thank God you're okay."

She moaned. She felt far from okay. Slowly she tested each limb and found them all attached and working. "My head hurts." Her tongue felt like an old rubber boot.

"You have a cut above your ear."

She lifted a heavy arm to check and found a thick bandage. She touched it gently and moaned at the pain even her light touch brought. "Am I all right?"

"Pretty much."

"How about you?"

He nodded. "A few bruises. Nothing to worry about."

She couldn't bring herself to ask about the plane.

"*Gracie Two* can be repaired."

She heard his disappointment and voiced her own. "There goes the money we made over the summer."

"It's not that bad. I can do most of the work."

A spasm of pain tore through her middle. She groaned and pressed her hands to her stomach. "I think I'm going to throw up."

Billy jerked around, somehow found a basin, and handed it to her.

She heaved up the contents of her stomach.

Billy took the basin out of the room. He returned with a wet cloth and sponged her face and hands.

Tears streamed from the outer corners of her eyes, dripping into her ears. "I feel awful."

He sat on the edge of the bed. "Doc says you will for awhile."

"You got the doctor?"

"You scared me half to death when you didn't come to right away."

She touched the bandage on her head again. "It's just a bang."

He nodded, his expression troubled.

"What is it?"

"Grace, why didn't you tell me we were going to have a baby?"

"A baby?" She pressed her flattened hands across her stomach. "I'm going to have a baby?" She laughed. "I can't believe it."

"You didn't know?"

She shook her head, grinning foolishly. "I wondered when Nellie said something about morning sickness, but I was only sick those few days when the house smelled so bad of mice. And my monthly business has always been so irregular." His dark eyes were guarded. A cold shudder raced across her shoulders. She began to shiver. "The baby is all right, isn't it?"

Billy's shoulders slumped. He took her cold hands in his warm grasp. "Grace, you lost the baby."

"No." A vicious shudder raked her body. "No." She pressed her hands to her face. A shrill keening filled the room.

It went on a full minute before Grace understood it came from her.

Billy wrapped his hands around hers, but she jerked away, turning her face to the wall.

The keening continued as if from a source outside herself.

"Grace, stop it." Billy's voice was strained. "Stop it, I say."

She took a deep breath, gritted her teeth; the sound ended. "Now look at me."

She turned her face toward him, but her eyes focused on a spot behind his eyes.

"We'll be okay."

Slowly she brought her gaze to him, seeing the pain and confusion in his eyes. But not feeling it. "I should never have gone flying." She ground the words out past aching teeth. "I should have stayed in Toronto with your parents. I would have been safe there."

Billy groaned. "I didn't mean for you to get hurt. You know that."

"I lost my baby." She turned to the wall and pulled the covers to her chin.

Billy waited for a minute, two, three, then he moaned. "Don't blame me, Gracie. Please don't blame me." When she didn't respond, he left the room.

After his footsteps faded, Grace stared at the wall. Her eyelids felt stretched; her eyes way too large.

She didn't want to think about what had happened—not about the accident, not about Billy, not about the baby. She didn't want to feel anything. She forced her eyes shut. Her lungs hurt. She took a shaky breath and concentrated on relaxing. Shivering, she pulled the covers closer. Mercifully, exhaustion allowed her to sleep.

When she awoke, the room lay in dusky shadows.

"I brought you some tea."

She nodded without looking at Billy. "Maybe later." She knew he stood waiting for her to look at him or say something, but it was all she could do to keep her insides from shattering into a million fragments. If she saw her pain reflected in his eyes, she knew she would come undone. So she stared at nothing, said nothing.

With a muffled groan, Billy left the room.

Grace turned on her side and again let sleep hide the terrors. She woke momentarily when Billy crawled in beside her. He said nothing to her, made no effort to put his arms around her. Instead, he turned his back and lay stiff.

She didn't move a muscle. If only he would hold her and let her cry against him.

He was gone when she awoke the next morning, bright sunlight pouring in the window.

A suffocating ache welled up inside, threatening to choke her. She moaned, forcing it back, pressing her flattened palms to her stomach, trying to relieve the pain. But the pain did not dwell in her stomach. It swelled in her heart. It overwhelmed her in a flood. Sobbing quietly, she lay very still, tears soaking her pillow.

Sometime later, her tears spent, her insides hollow, she lay staring at the ceiling, seeing nothing, feeling nothing.

Billy returned at noon and brought in a tray with tea and biscuits. "Grace, you need to eat something."

But she turned her back to him and did not answer.

Several times during the day, she heard him tiptoe to the bedroom. Each time she pretended to be asleep, but toward evening, he stood over the bed, waiting for her to open her eyes.

"I knew you weren't sleeping." He sighed. "You can't pretend forever. You haven't eaten anything all day. I've made some soup. I want you to eat a bit of it."

He waited until she felt compelled to answer if only to get him to leave her alone. "I'm not hungry."

"So eat only a little bit. It will give you strength."

Strength for what? she wondered. *To get up and make a mess of my life again?*

"Grace." His voice was stern. "You can't let this beat you."

Why not? she thought, but she only looked at him without blinking.

In the end, she took a few spoonfuls of the soup and drank some tea simply to avoid arguing.

Next morning, Billy stood at the side of the bed. "Are you getting up today, Grace?"

She opened heavy eyes and squinted at him. "I'm very tired," she whispered.

He nodded. "Fine. You rest." He looked like he wanted to say more, but Grace closed her eyes, too weary to care.

After awhile, she lost track of time, wanting nothing more than to escape into sleep where her thoughts could not bother her.

If only Billy wouldn't keep coming in and out, she could sleep forever, she fumed, after yet another visit and an attempt to get her to eat.

❧

"I heard about your troubles."

Grace jerked around to stare at Willow.

"I brung you some things." Her eyes, dark and steady, rested on Grace. "You be needing some healing."

Tears flooded Grace's eyes.

Willow stepped into the room. "I made my special tea for ya." She set an open pot and a cup on the dresser. "But first, ya need to wash up. Whilst you sit yerself up, I'll bring ya some water."

Before Grace could voice her protest and explain she didn't feel up to it, Willow turned from the room, returning almost immediately with a pan of water and a cloth. Leaning over, she wrapped a strong, warm arm behind Grace's shoulders and pulled her forward.

"I'll just put another pillow behind ya." With gentle hands, she washed Grace's face with the warm cloth, patting it dry. She washed each hand carefully.

Grace stared at her helplessly. "You don't need to do this."

"It's what I'm best at: caring for the sick and hurting."

"I don't deserve it."

Willow straightened and frowned. "And why would ya be not deserving a little human kindness?"

Grace shook her head, unable to speak.

Willow finished. "I lost three babies before I had my Zeke. Some babies come for but a moment. Their visit is so short we don't even get to know them." She sat at the edge of the bed, her gaze on a distant spot.

She had Grace's attention, though Grace wondered if Willow had forgotten her in remembering her own pain and loss.

"There is no place on earth where I remember my lost babies except here." She pressed a hand to her chest, then spun around to face Grace. "Your baby will always be there." She nodded once. "And you will always miss her."

A jolt raced through Grace's body. "Her?"

Willow nodded as if that was all the explanation Grace needed. Again, her eyes focused on a place in her memories. "I named my babies. Sarah, Martha, and Joshua."

Grace digested this bit of information, never questioning that Willow had known there were two girls and a boy. "I think I'd like to name my baby."

Willow nodded.

Grace thought about it a moment. "I want to name the baby after my mother, Eleanor May." She smiled. "Do you think my mother is holding my baby?"

Willow smiled. "Of course. Now I want ya to drink this tea." She poured dark liquid from the pot and handed the cup to Grace. "This will be making ya feel right again."

Grace sniffed at the brew, wrinkling her nose.

"Go ahead. It will help ya."

Grace took a swallow and shuddered. "It doesn't taste like it will make me feel better."

"It will."

Grace took three more gulps and paused. "I wish everything could be made right by a swallow or two of this stuff."

Willow's eyes narrowed. "Ya not be meaning the baby."

Her face feeling stiff, Grace let her gaze slip away from Willow's dark, knowing eyes. "I've said things to Billy I shouldn't have," she whispered. "I know it wasn't his fault." If blame was to be placed, it was her fault. For not refusing to fly with him, for not knowing she was pregnant, for being so incompetent.

Willow took the cup from her and pulled her into her arms. Grace sobbed against the thin shoulders as Willow patted her back and clucked comfortingly. "Crying is the best thing for ya," she said as Grace's sobs subsided.

Grace pulled away, laughing a little. "Then I guess I must be doing all right. It seems I've done nothing but cry these past days."

Willow nodded. "There's healing in tears. Women have that; men, they have to find another way."

"Maybe you're right." She hadn't given much thought to how Billy felt about the loss of the baby. He'd said nothing since that first day when he seemed more upset that she hadn't told him than about the baby's loss.

Willow stood, her hands on her hips. "It's time ya be getting out of bed."

Grace gaped at her. "Now?"

"It's been long enough. The longer ya lay around, the harder it will be." She pulled open a drawer. "What ya wanting to wear?"

It was easier to tell her than to argue, so Grace found herself helped into clean clothes.

"Now ya swing yer legs over the side and sit a mite. Ya might find yerself shaky for a spell."

With Willow at her side, Grace did as instructed, clutching her head when it spun with dizziness.

Willow waited quietly, then took Grace's arm. "Now ya walk to the sofa and sit."

With legs quivering like saplings, Grace hobbled to the front room and sank to the sofa, sweat beading her brow, her breathing ragged.

"That's fine. Now I've put some food in the cellar—roast chicken, potato salad, some fresh greens—all ya have to do is set it on the table." She handed the cup of brew to Grace. "Finish this up. It'll do ya good." She waited for Grace to drain the cup and hand it to her. "Now I'll be going. Ya'll feel better every day and soon be right as ya can be."

"Thank you, Willow." Tears stung her eyes. "You've been so helpful."

After Willow left, Grace sat on the sofa, wondering if her legs would carry her to the chair where she'd left a book. She grimaced. It was either that or return to bed, and suddenly the bedroom seemed stifling. Gritting her teeth, she pushed to her feet and hobbled to the chair, pausing as she retrieved the book, surprised at how steady her legs seemed. Willow had proved correct. Whatever she'd put into that bitter brew, Grace could already feel improvement in her strength.

Engrossed in her book, she didn't hear Billy enter the house until he stood before her. She slammed the book shut and stuck it behind the cushion.

"I'm glad to see you're up. You are feeling better, aren't you?"

"Yes, I am. Willow came over and made me some herbal tea. It seems to have helped."

Billy nodded. "I'm glad." He pulled the chair close and studied her carefully. "Grace, I. . ." He hesitated.

Grace held up a hand, having made up her mind to clear the air between them. "Billy, I don't blame you for what happened. It was my fault entirely. I knew I shouldn't go flying with you. It was only because I had watched you day after day and it looked like such fun." She shrugged. "But I guess one of us has to keep their feet on the ground." She hurried on while she had the strength, ignoring the wary look in his eyes. "And if I weren't so stupid, I would have known I was going to have a baby." She studied her hands.

Billy blew air over his lips. "Grace, why must you always blame yourself? Why can't you see that life isn't out to prove you incompetent or stupid? It isn't your fault anymore than it's mine. It was an accident. Pure and simple."

He took her hands. "Gracie, look at me." He waited until she complied. "You are not stupid. You are not to blame." He shook his head. "I don't understand why you feel this way about everything."

"I don't." She wasn't even sure what he was talking about, but it seemed best to deny it.

"Yes, you do. Like this book." He retrieved it.

She looked down, trying to hide the blush she felt racing up her cheeks.

"See, you're getting all hot and bothered." He tipped her chin up with his finger. "Why do you try and hide your reading?"

She shook her head. How could she explain how guilty she felt when he caught her with a book? As if she didn't have something more useful to do.

"I'm not going to scold you or question you about your work. Far as I'm concerned, you can do what you want about cooking and cleaning and all that sort of thing. I'm happy just having you here. I'm not looking for some sort of slave."

She searched his eyes. Somehow she was certain he didn't mean it. Not that she thought he wanted a slave, but she knew he would expect something from her besides being around for company. Finally, she shook her head. "I'm your wife. I'm supposed to do things."

He sighed. "You do things enough. I don't care if you make bread or buy it. I don't care if you grow a garden or buy canned goods from Mr. Tunney. Do you think I care if you enjoy reading?" He shook her a little. "Can't you see, I want you to be happy? I want you to enjoy doing things for me, not because you think I or someone else expects it of you."

She shook her head. "It's not that easy."

He pushed to his feet. "It is if only you'd believe it." He shoved his hand through his hair. "But if you choose not to believe it, then there's nothing I can say to prove otherwise."

"No, I suppose not." She refused to meet his glance, knowing she had somehow disappointed him. Again.

❧

The days passed. Grace slowly found her strength returning, though inside she felt dead, lifeless.

One day, a deep longing pulled at her. She wandered around, poking at a picture of Irene and one of her father, both so far away. She turned and picked up a book, but it held no appeal. She looked out the window. Suddenly, the outdoors called, and she hurried out. She needed to do something, but all she felt was a strange, restless urging.

A cluster of trees stood tall and straight in the far corner of the yard, past the barn. Having wandered there a few times, she knew that wild roses grew there in abundance. It was the perfect spot, and she gathered up several large rocks, carrying them to it. The sun beat down on her head. Sweat soon drenched her, but still she trundled back and forth with rocks until she had a small pile. Birds whistled and chattered; a crow flew overhead scolding. The leaves whispered as she arranged the rocks into a neat rectangle, then sat back on her heels to study her work.

"Good-bye, little Eleanor, my sweet baby. I never got a chance to know you, but still I miss you. I will never forget you."

The little mound of rocks seemed so inadequate, but it was all she could think to do.

"Grace, what are you doing?"

Billy's soft-spoken words directly behind her made her jerk her head up.

"It's for the baby," she murmured.

He sank down on his knees beside her. "What do you mean?"

"Willow told me how she lost three little babies. She said she named them. So I named our baby Eleanor May after my mother." A thought struck her and she turned to face him. "I hope that's all right with you. I never thought to ask."

His dark eyes glistened. "I like that." His words were husky. "Little Eleanor May."

She turned back to the mound. "I wanted something to

remember her by." She paused and took a deep breath, knowing she would never need a remembrance. "Maybe what I really wanted was a way to say good-bye." She nodded toward the rocks. "It isn't a grave, really, but it's the only way I know of saying a proper good-bye."

She reached for Billy's hand. They clung to each other.

"Good-bye, Baby," Billy whispered.

"Good-bye," Grace echoed. She turned to Billy, surprised to see how his eyes glistened. It was her undoing. She flung herself into his arms, sobbing.

"Gracie, Gracie," he murmured, his tears merging with hers.

eight

"I didn't know if I should come." Nellie hesitated in the doorway.

"Why ever not?" Grace asked.

Nellie pressed her hands against her swollen middle and nodded toward Grace's flat stomach. "Me so pregnant, and you. . ."

"Don't be silly. I'm glad for you. Come on in."

Nellie called over her shoulder to Tom. "Pick me up when you're done in town." She turned back to Grace. "I've been wanting to come since I heard."

"I'm glad you've come."

"Grace, I'm so sorry." She hugged Grace as close as she could with her rounded tummy.

Grace laughed as the baby kicked a protest. "It's all right, Baby," she murmured. "I'm not hurting your mama." She wished she could take Nellie out and show her the memorial for her lost baby. Billy had fashioned a wooden cross with the words "Baby Eleanor" carved in the crosspiece, but Nellie looked as if the walk would be too much. Besides, Grace admitted, she wasn't sure how others would feel about what she and Billy had done.

"I have prayed for you every day," Nellie added, waddling to the table and sitting down. "I can't imagine how one would deal with such a loss apart from God's help."

Grace busied herself making tea. God seemed to have withheld His help in her situation. She sought some other topic. "Willow was here a few days ago. She made me the most vile tea and said it would make me feel better."

Nellie laughed. "And did it?"

Grace gave a weak grin. "I started to gain my strength back after that."

Nellie cocked her head. "But did it make you feel better?"

Grace tried to smile, but it wobbled. She tightened her lips. "Will I ever feel better?" she whispered.

Nellie looked thoughtful. "I guess I don't know if you'll ever be able to think about this without hurting, but I think you will heal in your heart even as your body is healing."

Grace nodded. "I want to believe you're right, but there are times I wonder if I'll ever. . ." She swallowed hard. Her fears sounded more like self-pity than anything.

"What is it you wonder?" Nellie prodded.

"Nothing. It was nothing."

For a moment, Nellie was silent, then she spoke low and soft. "Grace, I can only guess at what you're thinking and feeling. I suppose you wonder if you'll get a chance to have another baby. Chances are you will."

Grace nodded. "Willow told me she lost three before Zeke was born."

"There you go. Look at her now."

Grace laughed. "I know, but Willow is such a good person. She knows all about raising a family and healing and everything."

Nellie gave her a strange look. "You're a good person, Grace."

Grace looked away. "I'm stupid and incompetent."

"Grace, how can you say that? I've been so impressed with how you learned to cope with so many new things. Why, I don't know how many times I said to Tom what an amazing person you are. You were thrown into a situation that would have sent most of us home crying to our mothers. This house! I said to Tom I think I would have refused to live in it, yet you got down to work and scrubbed it until it shines." She waved her hand around the room. "No one would know this was the same place."

She paused to catch her breath. "You learned everything

there was to learn in almost no time. You even learned how to drive." She shook her head. "I could never do that."

Grace listened to all her friend said without answering.

"So why do you think so poorly of yourself?"

"I don't think I do. I'm only being honest."

Nellie looked at her long and serious. "I think you're afraid of something, but I don't have any idea what or why you should be. All I can do is pray for you. I know God will find a way of showing you how precious and worthwhile you are to Him."

Grace jerked upright. "What did you say?"

"When?"

"Just now. This very minute."

"About asking God to show you how precious and worthwhile you are?"

"You said 'to Him.'"

"Yes, of course I did. Don't you know how much He loves you?"

Grace shook her head. "I suppose so. I believe Jesus died to provide a way of salvation."

Nellie's eyes narrowed. "And after that?"

Grace shrugged. "I doubt I'll ever be able to live up to His standards."

"Like what?"

"You know, love one another, don't lie, be patient, gentle, kind, and all those sorts of things."

Nellie shook her head. "It sounds to me like you think you have to earn God's approval—His love."

Grace thought about that. "He says we should obey Him. I seem to be always failing someplace or other. Sometimes I think I'm too stupid to figure it all out."

"Grace, there was nothing you could do to earn your salvation, and there is nothing you can do to earn God's love. There is nothing you can do to make Him love you more, nothing you can do to make Him love you less."

Grace thought about Nellie's words. It just wasn't that simple.

Thankfully, Nellie realized she'd said enough and turned to other topics. "By the way, Mrs. Paige stopped me in town and said she thought you could use some more books." Nellie dug into her bag and handed two to Grace.

After Nellie's visit, Grace did her best to pick up the threads of her life.

"I'll be the best wife you could ask for," she told Billy.

"You're already the best wife I could ask for."

Grace shook her head. "I don't know how to garden, can meat, or butcher." The news of an upcoming butcher ring had her in a panic.

Billy laughed. "Grace, how many times do I have to tell you: What you don't know you can learn." He cocked his head. "Do you suppose all the women you know were born knowing how to do what they do?"

"I'll bet they were."

He grabbed her and hugged her. "You know they weren't. And if you'd allow yourself to be honest, you'd admit you can do just about anything you put your little head to."

"I can try," she said rather dubiously.

"Gracie, my wife, it's about time you grew up. You're no longer a child being smothered by your sister and father."

His words stung. "They didn't smother me. They only wanted to protect me."

"I ask myself over and over what it was they were protecting you from. Someone like me, perhaps, who would see you as a perfectly capable adult? One, I might add—" he rubbed noses with her—"who I want to spend the rest of my life with." He pulled away. "Now, I think *Gracie Two* is ready to fly again. I'm going to take her for a test run. Want to watch?"

Grace's heart clenched at the thought of him going up again. Secretly, she'd hoped he wouldn't be able to repair the airplane. But day after day he disappeared into the barn, pounding and hammering as he forged ahead with repairs.

She shuddered. "I don't think I can bear to watch." She ran inside and grabbed up a book, forcing her mind to the words on the pages, but when she heard the plane take off, she couldn't take it and hurried outside to watch Billy put the craft through her paces. She waited and watched until he landed safely. Only then was she able to fill her lungs without discomfort.

Billy hurried to her side, smiling. "She's as good as new. Now I can get back to work." He pulled her close, not noticing her resistance.

After lunch the next afternoon, a young boy rode into the yard.

Billy came out of the barn as Grace stepped from the house.

The boy skidded to a halt before Grace. "Mr. Deans asked me to bring you a message, Ma'am. He says to tell you Mrs. Deans is asking for you."

Grace clenched her hands together.

"Thank you, Son." Billy stepped to Grace's side.

The boy waved and rode away.

Grace clutched Billy's arm. "It must be time for the baby."

"You best go see. I'll bring the car to the step."

Grace took a moment to grab her handbag and a kerchief to throw over her hair. Billy had the car waiting when she stepped outside.

"You don't suppose she's having trouble, do you?"

He shook his head. "Probably she only wants someone to stay with her while Tom goes for the doctor."

"Of course. That's probably it."

She stepped toward the car, then turned back to Billy. "If there's anything wrong, I don't know anything about helping a baby be born."

He patted her hand. "You go see what she wants. You'll be just fine."

She nodded as she drove away. Life was always so easy for Billy. If only she could have half the self-assurance he did.

She jerked to a stop in front of the Deaness' house.

Tom met her at the door. "I'm glad you could come. She's in labor." He rubbed his hair.

Grace gave him a quick glance. He looked like he was

the one in labor, his eyes red rimmed, his hair tossed up, his skin pale.

"She's through there." He pointed to the bedroom. "Now you're here, I'm going for the doc. I think it's time."

"Time. You mean the baby is almost here?"

"It's been going on long enough."

"How long?"

"She's been laboring hard since night before last."

"Oh my." Grace rushed through the door. She might not know anything about babies, but that seemed an awfully long time. "Is she all right?" But one glance at Nellie told her the poor woman was close to exhaustion, her face flushed from exertion, her eyes hollow, her hair matted with sweat.

"You go get Doc straightaway," she called over her shoulder, then bent close to Nellie. "It's me, Nellie. How are you doing?"

Nellie's eyelids fluttered open. "You're here. Grace, pray for me. The baby isn't coming right."

Grace drew back. Pray? Apart from church, she seldom prayed. She wasn't even sure she knew how. But she couldn't deny Nellie's desperate plea. "Of course, I'll pray," she agreed.

"Pray out loud so I can hear you. I don't seem to have the strength to do it myself."

Grace could barely hear Nellie's whispered words. How could she deny Nellie's request? "God, help us." The words, the best she could come up with, sounded empty, plain. But a spasm gripped Nellie, and there wasn't time to think of it any longer.

The pain seemed to go on and on. Just when Grace wondered if Nellie could take any more, it eased, though she could see Nellie was not comfortable.

"Water," Nellie mumbled.

Grace held the glass to her friend's mouth so she could drink. When Nellie fell back against the pillows, Grace found a cloth and wiped her face. Before she was done, another pain wrenched Nellie into a half-sitting position. She bit her lip so hard it bled. A long, thin scream edged through Nellie's clenched teeth. Again, Grace feared the pain would be more than Nellie could endure. Again, it subsided only to grip her again. And again.

Afternoon had given way to evening. The room grew shadowed, and Grace lit a lamp, wondering when Tom would return. He'd been gone far too long. She heard a noise and looked up from holding Nellie, trying to ease her through another pain, to see Tom at the door, a look of fear on his face.

She signaled him that they'd talk in the other room and hurried out to hear what he had to say.

"The doc's away out of town. I couldn't find him." His voice crackled with tension.

"What are we going to do? I don't know how much more she can take."

As if to prove her point, Nellie screamed, a sound that went on and on, tearing through Grace's brain.

Tom shuddered. "I don't know."

A sudden thought came to Grace. "Go get Willow Welty. She'll know what to do. Hurry."

Tom raced from the room before Grace finished speaking.

Taking a deep breath, Grace returned to Nellie's side. If only she knew how to help her friend. That last pain seemed to have taken the final remnant of Nellie's strength, and she lay limp, barely able to moan as another pain assailed her body.

Grace shook her head. How much more could Nellie and the baby endure?

She was so grateful to hear Tom return and the sound of Willow's voice. She leapt up and hurried to greet them, grabbing Willow's arm and half dragging the woman to the bedroom. "Hurry, she's so weak."

Willow stepped to Nellie's side, probed at Nellie's stomach, then straightened.

"Grace, go boil some water. I want to give her something to drink."

Grace hurried to do as told.

When she returned, Willow had turned Nellie to one side

and was massaging Nellie's stomach.

Willow saw Grace with hot water. "Good, take that packet and pour it in a cup. Fill it with the water."

Grace obeyed.

"Help me sit her up."

Together, they dragged Nellie up, and Willow held the cup to her lips. "Have some of this, Dearie. It will get ya right."

Weakly, Nellie downed the drink.

"Now help me," Willow murmured to Grace.

"I don't know what to do."

"Just do as I say."

And Grace did. She moved Nellie, held her while Willow worked over her, ran for more rags when a gush of blood flooded the bed. Her limbs seemed to function apart from her mind.

"Now give one more push," Willow told Nellie. "Come on, Girl, one more."

Nellie screamed once and collapsed. Willow scooped up a baby. "Come on, little one. Breathe." She wiped the mouth and nose and rubbed the little chest gently.

Grace stared at the tiny, motionless body, willing the infant to live.

The baby squirmed and gave a faint meowing sound.

"That's it. Try harder." Willow tweaked the soles of the tiny feet. The infant jerked back and wailed. "Thank God. Thank God," Willow muttered. "This little gal has a fighting spirit. She'll go far, mark my words."

She thrust the baby into Grace's arms.

Grace gulped at how slippery the newborn was. Willow handed her a clean rag. "Hold the baby while I take care of the rest."

Grace barely noticed as Willow cut the cord, her attention focused on the newborn in her hands. So tiny. So complete. So loud.

Willow wrapped a cloth around the baby. "Hold her close while I tend to the mother."

Half an hour later, Willow straightened. "She'll be fine now."

Then she showed Grace how to wash the baby.

It was so wonderful and new.

On her way home, despite the warm morning sun, Grace started to shake. By the time she reached the house, she could barely drive.

Billy rushed out to greet her. "Is everything all right?"

Her teeth chattered so she couldn't answer. Billy sprang to her side. "Is Nellie. . . ?"

Grace nodded. "Fine."

"The baby?"

"Fine." She gulped again.

"Then what on earth is the matter? You look like someone died, at the very least."

She burst into tears, sobs shuddering her entire body.

Billy lifted her from the car and held her in his arms, shepherding her toward the house, where he led her to the sofa and pulled her down beside him, enclosing her in his arms.

She leaned against him, letting her helplessness consume her.

"Gracie, what's happened? What's the matter?"

She rolled her head back and forth. "They almost died," she managed to wail. "I didn't know what to do." Suddenly it poured out. "The baby wouldn't come. And Doc was away. I didn't know what to do. All I could think was to send for Willow. At least she knew what to do." She shuddered. "Otherwise I'm sure both Nellie and the baby would have died." A sob choked her words. "And it would have been my fault. Just like when my baby died. And my mother." She knew before she'd finished speaking that her words made no sense, yet they were the head and tail of the great fear and guilt she experienced at every new challenge.

Billy stiffened. "Wait a minute. Didn't you tell me it was your idea to get Willow?"

She nodded against his shoulder, her tears dried by the hollowness of her heart.

"That was pretty smart. Seems to me you maybe saved

both their lives." He held her tightly. "Grace, as long as you insist on assigning blame about our baby, you condemn me as much as yourself. You have to accept it was an accident. No one was to blame."

Again she nodded. She knew that. In her head. It was harder to convince her heart. She felt Billy's deep sigh and knew he wasn't going to let the rest of it go. She had no one to blame but herself. She should have bitten her tongue before she uttered the words.

"Now, what's this about your mother?"

He waited, but she remained silent.

"I thought she died when you were several months old."

She managed a nod.

He turned and grasped her by both shoulders, giving her a little shake. "Then what's this nonsense about being to blame?"

At first she refused to meet his eyes, then as he waited, she took a deep breath. "Irene told me Mother never got over having me. She said Mother should not have had me." She stared into Billy's eyes, aching to find understanding there, perhaps even absolution.

"Ah, Gracie, what a burden you carry." He pulled her to his chest, cradling her tenderly. "I don't know why Irene would say such a thing, but how can you blame yourself? It was a choice you had nothing to do with."

"I know that. I've told myself over and over. But it didn't help. It doesn't change the way I feel in here." She pressed a balled-up fist to her chest. "I know it doesn't make sense, but I can't help it. I still feel like I did something very wrong. Somehow it's my fault my mother died." Her voice fell to a whisper. "I can never make up for it."

He stroked her hair, pressing her head closer. "So nothing you do is ever good enough."

She stiffened. How had he read her inmost thoughts?

"Grace, sooner or later, you are going to have to believe in yourself."

She sat up and faced him. His eyes so tender and encouraging almost made her forget the doubts lurking in the darkness of her soul. Almost. For a moment. Then reality stamped its foot. She couldn't forget how inept she was when Nellie needed her; how her own foolishness had resulted in the loss of her baby; how she had never known her mother because Mother never got over Grace's birth.

Her shoulders sagged. "You see me the way you want me to be. I have to live with what I really am."

"I think I see you clearly. It is you who have your vision clouded by whispers and doubts that don't even make sense."

"Perhaps." She was too tired to argue. She'd been up all night with Nellie. All she wanted now was to go to bed. "I'll make some breakfast."

"I already ate." He pulled her to her feet and led her toward the bedroom. "You look all in. Go to sleep. Things will look better when you're rested." He waited for her to pull off her clothing, soiled with her night's labors and smelling of sweat— hers and Nellie's together. She sank into the bed and sighed.

Billy pulled the covers around her shoulders, kissed her brow, and tiptoed from the room.

❧

That evening over supper, Grace caught Billy's watchful gaze upon her more than once.

"Nellie had a baby girl. Willow made me hold her. It's the first time I held a baby." She smiled. "I had no idea they were so small."

She bustled back and forth between the stove and the table. "Once Tom knew Nellie was fine, he couldn't take his eyes off the baby. He grinned so wide it must have hurt."

"Grace," Billy began.

She knew he wanted to say more about their conversation earlier in the day, but she'd tucked the whole affair back into its hidden chamber. *It's not hidden any longer,* a persistent voice warned. But Grace ignored the inner arguments, even as she forestalled Billy's questions.

"Billy, have you ever held a baby?"

He shook his head. "Not a little one."

She laughed, ignoring its mocking echo. "We'd make quite a pair, wouldn't we? Neither of us knows anything about babies."

"Nobody's born knowing. What you don't know—"

"You can learn. I know. I know." She set the bowl of boiled potatoes at his elbow and sat down across from him.

He gave her a steady look. "You can't run forever, Grace."

She blinked. "Who's running? Pass the butter, please."

"Fine." But his stern expression warned her he wouldn't be forgetting it.

❧

A few days later, Old Len drove into the yard. "Got a message for Mr. Marshall."

"What is it?" Billy came from the barn, wiping his hands on a rag.

Old Len handed a folded piece of paper to Billy.

Billy stuffed the oily rag into his back pocket and opened the note.

"Mr. Tunney said it was from that oil man you give a ride to awhile back." Old Len leaned forward, curiosity written in every wrinkle.

"Yes, it is. He wants me to fly him again." Billy looked up from the piece of paper. "Thank you, Len."

"You want to be sending a reply?"

"I'll be going to town to use the phone myself."

"Oh." He sat back in disappointment. "I'll be heading back then."

Billy waved, waiting for Len to turn onto the main road before walking over to Grace. "Mr. Boushee wants to hire me."

Grace blinked. "What does he want you to do?"

Billy stuffed the note in his pocket. "He wants to go up north to Norman Wells."

Grace studied her husband's face, seeing the way he shuffled his feet and shifted his gaze past her left ear. "So why the nervousness?"

Billy grinned. "Can't fool you for a minute." He shrugged.

"Norman Wells is way up north. We'd have to take the trip in steps. Then I'd have to stay with him until he's ready to come back."

"How far north?"

"Up the Mackenzie River in the Northwest Territories. A long ways."

Grace's mind raced, trying to assess what exactly Billy's news meant. "How long would you be gone?"

"A week, maybe two."

Her mouth fell open. She stared. He might as well have said he was going to the North Pole. On second thought, maybe he was.

"What about me?"

It was his turn to look startled. "What do you mean?"

"What am I supposed to do for two weeks while you're gone?"

He shrugged. "Whatever you like. Read. Rest. Go see Nellie and the new baby."

She mentally shuddered. Although she longed to see her friend and the new baby, something inside cringed at the thought of facing Nellie and seeing the accusation in her gaze.

"You could even go see Irene if you wanted. Take the train."

She shook her head. "Irene doesn't have room for me. Besides, it's too far."

Billy laughed. "You came across the ocean. You came three thousand miles across Canada, but the idea of a three-hundred-mile trip to see your sister makes you tuck in your tail and hide."

Grace smiled. "I'll go another time." It wasn't the distance that hindered her; it was knowing she'd have to face again the guilt she had discovered lurking in her heart.

Billy slapped his thigh. "I have to go to the store and call Red."

"When will you leave?"

"Tomorrow morning, I guess. The sooner we're on the way,

the better Red will like it." He headed for the car. "I'll be back shortly."

An hour passed before Grace heard the car putt into the yard—an hour in which she had gone over every possible crisis she could encounter while he was away, an hour in which to imagine all sorts of accidents and disasters for Billy. The north! Where men froze to death; where bears lurked about, waiting for a chance for a free lunch. She shuddered. Only by gritting her teeth would she be able to let him go without getting hysterical.

He bounced into the house. "It's all set." He rubbed his hands together. "Man, this is the chance I've been waiting for. A big job, an important customer. This could put our business on its feet for good." He rubbed his palms some more, the sound grating over Grace's nerves. "I've always wanted to go up north. I've heard so much about it."

Grace turned back to supper preparations, her own worries buried deep in her mind.

The next morning, having made arrangements to meet Mr. Boushee in Edmonton, Billy prepared for an early start. "I'll phone the store every day and leave a message for you." He threw his satchel of clothing in the plane. "Of course, when I really get north, I probably won't have access to a phone." In went heavy mittens and a coat.

"You won't run into snow, will you?"

"Red says the north is unpredictable this time of year. His advice was to come prepared for anything."

"That's comforting," she muttered.

"We'll be fine. Red's been there before."

"Yes, that's reassuring, I suppose."

"Yup." He totally missed her sarcasm. "That's the works, I think." He nodded. "I guess I'm ready."

Suddenly, the enormity of what lay ahead hit her. "I'll be all alone." Panic laced her voice.

He took her in his arms. "Yes, Grace, you'll manage just fine. You have the car. You can do as you like."

She bit her tongue to keep from saying what she'd like was for him to stay home where they'd both be safe. "I can't bear to think of you being gone so long." She shivered. "And all the things that could go wrong."

"Then don't think about it. You can't make things any better or worse by dreading them."

She wanted to say it worked both ways: He couldn't make things better by assuming nothing but the best. Instead, she held him tight. It would be the last time she hugged him for two weeks—maybe more—and she wanted to store up the feel of him.

He kissed her. Nothing mattered but having her arms around him. With a muffled groan, he pulled away. "I have to go. Red is waiting." He bent for one last, quick kiss. "I'll miss you, Gracie One."

Tears stinging her eyes, she stepped back, waving as he took off. She stared into the sky until he vanished from sight.

nine

He hadn't been gone fifteen minutes when the house felt as hollow as an empty tin can. Even the cat and her kittens had wandered away and didn't come when she called.

"I will not be a baby," she vowed aloud, shrinking back as her words echoed in the stillness. "What would Nellie do?"

That was easy. Nellie had a new baby to care for.

"Well, what about Willow?"

Again, the answer was simple. Willow had her brood of youngsters, a huge garden, her chickens, and her herbs. Willow probably never had time to sit, let alone to wonder how to pass the time.

"What about Irene?"

She didn't know. It was weeks since she'd heard from Irene, though she knew her sister had her plate full with a veteran and his motherless children to care for. "A tough row to hoe," Father would have said. For a moment, she contemplated visiting Irene as Billy had suggested. Then she shook her head. Seeing Irene, observing how competent she was, remembering the words she'd said to Grace so long ago—it was long ago. She'd only been a child. Time enough to forget it.

She sighed. If only one could forget things that easily.

The whole day stretched ahead of her empty and hollow. She'd avoided visiting Nellie since the baby's birth, but now loneliness made her feelings of guilt and inadequacy fade in comparison.

"I'll go before I change my mind," she muttered, hurrying to the car and driving away.

No one came to the door when she drove into the Deanses' yard. She saw Tom stacking hay in a field away from the house. Knocking but not waiting for an answer, she opened the door.

Loud wails filled the room.

"Nellie," she called softly, thinking Nellie might be putting the baby to sleep.

When there was no answer, she called louder, "Nellie!" Then she followed the sound to the front room.

Nellie, her head tipped back, a squalling, red-faced infant in her arms, sat limply in the rocker.

Grace smiled. She'd been expecting to see the picture of serene motherhood, not this look of utter exhaustion.

"Nellie," she spoke softly.

Nellie cracked open her eyes. "Hello, Stranger."

Grace smiled crookedly. "I didn't know if you'd want to see me again so soon."

Nellie's eyes widened. "I've been dying to see you and thank you for saving my life. Mine and little Rebecca's. Tom said he didn't know what to do. He said it was your idea to send for Willow." She held out a hand to Grace. "I owe you so much."

Grace sank to a chair. "I thought you would be angry."

"Angry? Why would I be angry?"

Grace shrugged and looked down. "I felt like I failed you. I didn't know how to help."

Nellie smiled. "Oh, Grace, you knew exactly what to do— get help." She waited until Grace met her eyes. "It was your resourcefulness that saved our lives."

The infant in Nellie's arms, quiet a moment while they talked, squalled angrily.

"Come and meet your namesake." Nellie turned the baby toward Grace. "This unhappy young lady is Rebecca Grace."

Grace touched her tentatively with her fingertip. "She's so soft. Does she cry like this all the time?"

Nellie sighed. "Occasionally she sleeps." She turned tired, desperate eyes to Grace. "Mostly she cries." She gulped. "I wish my mother was here." To Grace's consternation, Nellie broke into tears.

"Nellie, what can I do to help?"

Around her sobs, Nellie managed to get out, "Hold the baby for awhile so I can get the kitchen clean, the diapers washed." She dashed away her tears. "Would you mind?"

It was Grace's turn to gulp. "I'll do my best."

"Sit here." Nellie pushed herself to her feet and waited for Grace to position herself before she placed the still-crying infant in her arms.

Grace stiffened as the baby cried harder. "What's the matter?"

Nellie laughed. "She doesn't like to be moved, the little monkey."

Grace hardly dared breathe.

Nellie patted her shoulder. "Relax. She won't break."

Grace tried to do as she was told.

"Now, if you don't mind, I'll get a few things done."

"Go ahead. I'll see if she'll settle."

"Do your best, but don't be surprised if she keeps up her racket."

Grace studied the wrinkled, wide-mouthed infant. "So you're Rebecca Grace?" She ran the back of her finger along the infant's cheek. "You don't seem very happy about it." The baby hiccoughed and stopped crying. "There, see it's not all that bad, is it?"

As if to prove her wrong, the little one took a deep breath and let it out in a long angry wail.

Grace sighed. "I don't think she likes me," she called to Nellie.

"Then she doesn't like me or Tom either. She slept the first two days after she was born, but she's done nothing but cry since then." Nellie sat down, sighing wearily. "I'm lucky if she let's me get an hour's sleep at a time. I am so tired."

"I could hold her while you have a nap." Grace half hoped Nellie would refuse, but Nellie jumped up.

"Oh, thank you, Grace. It's just what I need." She hurried from the room, pausing only long enough to say, "It's not long since she's eaten. She should be all right for an hour or so."

Grace stared after her, then down at the crying infant. She

ried rocking, but the baby only stopped crying for a moment. Gingerly, lest she do something wrong, Grace shifted the baby to her shoulder. Again, a brief pause while she caught her breath, then more crying.

"You certainly know how to make me feel inadequate," she muttered. Unable to bear the distressed sounds any longer, she pushed to her feet, bouncing the infant in her arms.

The baby's cries settled to intermittent sobs. A minute later Grace saw the infant had fallen asleep. But when Grace tried to sit, the baby fussed so she kept moving, afraid if she stopped, the baby's cries would disturb Nellie.

Nellie woke up some time later. "She's sleeping?"

"As long as I keep walking. If I stop, she starts to fuss again." As if on cue, little Rebecca opened her eyes and wailed.

Nellie took her. "She'll be hungry now." She put the baby to her breast and turned back to Grace. "I can't thank you enough. You have no idea how tiring it is to look after her."

Grace flexed her sore arms. "Just an hour of it, and my arms ache."

Nellie nodded. "It makes me feel so helpless. Why doesn't she settle? Am I doing something wrong?"

Her questions burned into Grace's heart. "I'm sure you're doing everything you should. Maybe she's simply a fussy baby."

"Maybe."

Nellie seemed unaffected by her words. Grace understood. How often had she blamed herself for things when others assured her she was doing her best?

She stayed awhile longer, helping Nellie prepare supper for Tom before she headed home. As she passed the crossroads, she stopped the car. Willow would know if there was anything more Nellie could do. She turned the car down the road toward the Weltys'.

"Nellie looks plumb wore out," she explained to Willow. "I was wondering if you could tell her if there is anything more she should do."

"Mary, ya finish frying this chicken. Dan'el, ya run and get my bag. Mister," she called to her husband, "I'm off to see about the new baby."

"You do that, Woman. I'll look after the youn'uns."

Grace glanced around. They all seemed to understand Willow's job took her away from them.

"If ya will give me a ride over, it would save a mite of time."

"I'll be glad to."

Clutching her bag close to her chest, her eyes wide with apprehension, Willow climbed up beside Grace on the leather seat.

"This will be far enough," she said at the crossroads. She patted Grace's hands before she stepped down. "Ya did good." With a wave, she strode away.

Grace stared after her, repeating her words. *Yes.* She nodded. *I guess I did do good.*

Next morning she arrived at the store as Mr. Tunney raised the blinds.

"Mrs. Marshall, good morning."

"Morning. Did my husband phone?"

"Matter of fact he did. He said he arrived at Peace River Crossing last night. Said he'd be there a day or two getting pontoons on the plane. Wait a minute. I wrote it all down for you." He disappeared inside, returning with a scrap of paper. "Said everything was going well and for you not to worry." He handed her the paper reluctantly. "Said he'd call again tonight."

"Thanks, Mr. Tunney." About to drive away, she thought of something. "What time did he call?"

The storekeeper rubbed his chin. "Believe it was about nine o'clock. The missus and me was about to turn the lights out."

"Thanks again." Too late at night to ask if she could wait for Billy's phone call.

She drove a block before she pulled over and read his note. Nothing more than Mr. Tunney had said, but she reread it several times before tucking it into her handbag.

At home she immersed herself in a novel, determined to survive the day on her own.

Next morning she again arrived at the store as Mr. Tunney opened the door.

"Morning, Mrs. Marshall. Got another note for you. Your husband says he probably won't be able to call for the next few days though. He's way up north, isn't he? Such a long way." He handed Grace the piece of paper. "You must be real proud of that man of yours."

"Yes, I'm very proud of him." Thanking him, Grace took the note and drove away without explaining her pride came not from Billy venturing up north but from Billy's character—his optimism, his unfailing good spirits, his kindness.

"I wish he were here to give me a shot of his optimism right now," she muttered. This being alone with nothing but one's thoughts gave her entirely too much time to dwell on her doubts and fears. Yesterday had been haunted by the loss of her baby. When she forced herself to think of something else, she'd been equally distressed by thoughts of her own mother's death.

The idea of spending another day alone was unbearable. She turned toward the Deanses'. Perhaps Nellie would welcome her offer of help.

Nellie shepherded her into the house, her fingers to her lips. "She's sleeping. Willow gave me something for her and showed me comfort measures. She told me not to worry about Rebecca crying so much. Some babies simply need to cry more than others."

Two pairs of eyes turned toward the sudden wail from the other room.

Nellie sighed. "At least she sleeps some of the time. By the way, thanks for sending Willow."

Grace followed Nellie to the baby's cradle.

Nellie nursed the baby, then cradled her in one arm as she did her work.

"Have you heard from Billy?"

Grace nodded. "I won't hear for a few days now."

"Do I detect a tremor in your voice?"

"Probably. I don't like staying alone."

"Worried?"

Grace shook her head. "My thoughts won't give me any peace."

Nellie's hands stilled. "Grace, I wish there was some way I could make you see that God's peace is a gift 'that passes all understanding.' That's from the Bible."

"I do too, but I guess I have to figure it out myself." Nellie made it sound so simple—as if all she had to do was say yes, please, and peace would suddenly envelop her heart.

"I suppose you do. Just don't waste too much time doing it."

"I won't." The promise was easily spoken, but she had no notion of how she'd fulfill it. Perhaps Nellie was wrong. Perhaps some people were destined for peace, others for inner turmoil.

Every day Grace checked for messages from Billy. Four days she turned away in disappointment, returning to a silent, empty house. On the fifth day, Mr. Tunney handed her a slip of paper. She didn't wait for him to tell her what it said but hurriedly drove away. She braked the car and unfolded the paper.

"Everything is well. I've had a lot of fun and excitement. Will tell you when I get home. Expect to arrive Monday."

She folded the note carefully and put it with the others in her bag. Two more days and her agony of loneliness would end.

She drove to church the next day, her heart longing for words of comfort and encouragement, and she found them there, but the lonely house soon enough drove them away.

She woke early Monday, jumped from bed, and hurried to the kitchen to mix up cookie dough. She hurried from the table to the stove to the washbasin. If she kept busy, the time would pass faster. All the while she listened for the distant drone of the airplane.

Twice she ran from the house, looking to the sky, and returned disappointed. The third time she thought she heard him she waited, straining until she was certain the noise was real, then hurried outside and spotted the dark spot in the sky that rapidly drew closer. Billy barely had time to taxi to a stop before she raced toward him. He jumped down and caught her in his arms, kissing her.

"I missed you, Gracie."

"Me too."

"I've lots to tell you. It was a wonderful experience. Only one thing wrong with it, and that was being away from you." He kissed her again, longer, more gently.

She held him tightly.

After a moment, he extracted himself from her arms. "I brought you something." He reached into the cargo area and pulled out a bundle wrapped in brown paper and tied with twine.

But her eyes devoured him. His dark brown eyes shone with excitement and satisfaction, his lips parted in a wide smile. He flipped off his helmet; his dark hair glistened in the sun. She wet her lips. "What is it?"

He laughed. "Unwrap it and see."

She struggled with the strings until he flicked open his pocket knife and cut through them. The paper fell open and she lifted the article. "It's a coat."

"A parka," he corrected. "Made by one of the Indian women near Norman Wells."

She shook it. It was fine, doe-colored leather trimmed with fancy beadwork and lined with soft fur. "It's wonderful. Thank you." She leaned over to kiss his mouth.

"Umm. You taste good." He draped an arm over her shoulders and turned her toward the house. "What have you been doing with yourself while I was gone?"

She told him about visiting Nellie. "She named the baby Rebecca Grace."

He chuckled. "Gracie Three."

"Your trip went well?"

"We had to put down unexpectedly on the lake when the motor stalled, but it was nothing. We landed smooth as could be, and I soon had the line cleaned out."

She shivered. "I'm glad you're back safe and sound." While he was gone, she had not allowed herself to think about the consequences if something happened to him up in the wilds, but now it was safe to acknowledge she'd been concerned. "I missed you."

He hugged her tighter. "You better."

❧

They settled into a routine. Billy had several day jobs, flying men and supplies to Turner Valley and Banff.

Fall slowly descended with cool, crisp mornings, longer nights, a full harvest moon, and the sound of geese overhead, flying south in formation.

A contentment settled into Grace's heart. Billy was home; life was good.

She visited Nellie often, growing more confident helping with Rebecca.

❧

"I'll take these," she told Mrs. Paige, plunking four books on the desk.

"I'll be right there." Mrs. Paige looked out the window, her attention caught by something.

Grace joined her. The window looked out on a side street—quiet yards to the left. A wagon trundled down Main Street. A block away ran the back alley of a row of shops tucked in behind the more prestigious Main Street businesses. One was a gambling place. There were other low-class establishments. She'd taken one look at the signs and avoided the street.

She saw what held Mrs. Paige's attention.

A huddled figure stood behind one of the buildings. Grace had seen enough to know the front of these businesses were painted gaudily, but no paint had been wasted to glorify the back. Bare boards, windows stuffed with newspaper, broken furniture stacked against the wall, it was enough to make her shudder.

She couldn't make out the age or sex of the huddled figure, but she saw the hand uplifted toward the bulk of a man standing on the sagging step, clutching at his shirt front.

Grace could feel the desperation in that gesture. The man shook the hand away.

Mrs. Paige snorted.

Grace glanced at her, surprised at the hardness in her expression. Then she turned back to the drama.

The begging form reached up again. Grace thought she heard a cry but knew it was only in her imagination.

Grace shivered as the big man planted his fists on his hips and glowered at the pleading figure before he ducked inside and slammed the door.

The other figure crumpled to the ground.

Mrs. Paige snorted again and turned away.

"Who is that?" Grace kept her eyes on the pathetic bundle on the ground.

"No one you would care to know about." Mrs. Paige marked the due date in the books and pounded them down on the desk.

"I'm curious, that's all."

"Don't bother yourself about the likes of them."

Grace knew from the way Mrs. Paige drew her lips into a tight line that she would learn nothing from this source. She determined she would find someone to tell her about the scene she'd witnessed. As she told Mrs. Paige, she was curious.

She asked at the post office.

"I make it a point to know nothing about that establishment," Mrs. Schofield said, her black eyes snapping. "In my opinion, they shouldn't even be allowed in town." She closed her mouth and would say no more.

Grace went to Church's store. She'd decided to be less direct in the hopes of eliciting more information. "I saw something this morning," she began.

Lou Church leaned forward. She liked to hear about other people.

"You know that place behind the mercantile?"

Lou drew back. "Hummph. Know more than I want to. That's a fact."

"It was the strangest thing."

Again Lou leaned forward, her eyes alight with interest. "What do you mean strange?"

"This big man was shaking his fist at some poor soul. Out in the back alley, mind." Grace pretended an interest in the display of hankies. "I've always liked pansies embroidered on a hankie."

Lou lifted her nose and sniffed a sound of such pure disdain that Grace stared at her. "Young Maggie Murphy no doubt." She sniffed again. "I wondered how long it would be before Big Ed threw her into the streets."

"You sound like you know this Maggie Murphy." Grace sounded only mildly interested.

"I know of her. Most everyone in town does. Why she came marching into town as bold as you please. Didn't waste no time trying to find a decent job. No, sir. She found Ed's place right off, and that's where she's been since."

"Ed's place? Hmm. What sort of place is that?" She fingered several of the hankies, then turned toward the row of white gloves.

"Why it's the sort of place that gives a town a bad name, if you know what I mean."

Grace nodded absently. She was beginning to get the picture of what sort of place Ed ran. "You're telling me this young Maggie went to work for him?"

Lou tossed her head. "She couldn't wait to walk into his back room."

It was on the tip of Grace's tongue to ask how Lou knew so much about what went on in Ed's place, but she knew such a question would bring an end to her attempt to gather more information. "Makes me wonder why Ed would throw her out like that."

"The baby."

Grace almost dropped the pair of gloves she held. She blinked hard to control her emotions. "A baby." She cleared her throat. "What baby?"

Lou lifted another tray of gloves from behind the counter. "You might like these. Fine kid leather. All handmade. Just the thing for a fine lady like yourself."

"They are nice. Soft as down." She pulled them on and held out her hands to admire them. "I could use a new pair of gloves. I'll take these." A small price to pay for having her questions answered. "You were saying about a baby?"

"Miss Maggie Murphy wasn't as smart as she thought. She got herself in the family way. I understand Ed made her work all along." She leaned close to whisper. "Can you imagine such a thing?"

Grace shook her head, her eyes wide, silently begging Lou to continue.

Lou nodded. "I heard she had herself a baby girl not three days ago. I expect Ed gave her a chance to get back on her feet before he threw her out." Lou's mouth puckered like a pickle. "She won't be much use to Ed now. Not with a baby and all."

Grace pressed down the shudder that clawed at her insides. She kept her voice soft, sounding only mildly interested. "What do you suppose will happen to them?"

Lou shrugged as she wrapped the gloves in a flat box and handed them to Grace. "I heard Maggie was sick. Wouldn't surprise me if she died. For sure no one in this town is going to offer to help her."

Grace swallowed hard, stilling her insides. "But what about the baby?"

Lou rang in the money Grace handed her and returned the change. "With no one to care for it, what else but it will die too? It's a mercy really. What kind of future is there for a child born in that situation?"

Grace grabbed up the change and rushed from the store. She threw the parcel on the seat of the car and threw the car into gear, driving home much faster than usual. She couldn't believe Lou's words. To think no one would lift a hand to help that poor girl and her child. That poor innocent baby.

She drove into the yard in a whirl of dust and jerked to a halt.

Billy stepped from the barn, a piece of metal rod in his hands. "What's your hurry?"

Grace sprang from the car. "Do you know who Maggie Murphy is?"

Billy gave her a strange look. "Seems to me I heard the name a time or two."

"Seems everyone knows about her but me." At some point during the drive home, Grace's shock had turned to red-hot anger. "Seems like everyone is judge and jury as well."

Billy stepped back from her fury. "What are you talking about, Grace?"

She closed the distance between them. "I'm talking about a young girl thrown out on the streets." She jabbed her finger in his direction. "Or should I say, into the alley." She jammed her fists on her hips. "The woman—Maggie—I could maybe understand. After all, she made some choices. Maybe she should have to face the consequences. But a baby? Why should the baby be thrown out like a piece of garbage—human garbage? As if she did something wrong." Her breathing was ragged. "As if some poor little baby can be held responsible for what adults do. Before she was even born, mind. It's not her fault in the least."

Billy's mouth hung open; his eyes wore a startled look. "Grace, I've never seen you so worked up."

She breathed hard. "It's the injustice of it. Imagine blaming a poor innocent baby."

His eyes narrowed. "Yes, imagine." His tone was dry.

"What are you saying?"

"I'm agreeing. How can a baby be blamed for anything? They can't make any choices."

"That's exactly what I mean."

"Seems to me we've had this conversation before."

She blinked. "We have?"

He nodded. "It seems a young woman I know is suffering

from a sense of guilt because of something her sister said that makes her feel like it was her fault their mother died when this young woman was only a baby. Seems to me I've asked how a baby could be to blame."

"You're meaning me."

He nodded. "Don't you see how unfair it is to blame a baby?"

Her heart ticked the seconds as she stared at him without answering. "It makes sense when I say it."

He chuckled. "But not when I say it?"

"I didn't say that."

"Then what did you say?"

She shook her head. "There seems a chasm between what I think and what I feel."

Billy pulled her to his chest. "Poor Gracie, it's hard having all your misconceptions shattered."

She clutched his shirtfront, smelling the oil and grease of his morning's labors and something more—the warm manly smell of him, smells that comforted and held her. "I hate to admit to wrong thinking," she mumbled against his shirtfront.

He laughed. "I wouldn't expect you to capitulate too quickly; not my Gracie."

She thumped his chest. "Are you calling me stupid? Or stubborn?"

"Let's settle for saying you like to be dedicated to your ideas."

She laughed, turning her face up to him. "Billy, you always set things straight, don't you?"

He grinned down at her. "Just call me Mr. Fix-it."

"I don't know what I'd do without you."

"You better not be trying to find out." He shook her gently.

Her laugh bubbled up from deep inside, a sensation as pleasurable as any she'd felt for a long time. She leaned back in his arms and let her laughter ring out.

He grinned down at her.

ten

Billy pushed back from the table. "Great meal, Grace, thanks."

"It was the best I could do." She glimpsed the annoyance in his expression. "Glad you liked it."

"That's better." He carried the dishes to the washbasin and poured boiling water over them, adding from the bucket to cool it off.

"I can wash up," she protested. He often helped with dishes, and it always made her feel guilty.

He gave her a hard look. "I'm not insinuating you aren't capable of doing it on your own. Maybe I like to share your company." He plunged his hands into the water. "Or maybe I just want to get the grease out from under my fingernails."

She laughed. "I knew there was some underlying reason."

"Actually. . ." He handed her a plate to dry. "There isn't. It's all for you."

She nodded. Neither of them spoke for a moment.

"It seems like someone should do something to help that young woman."

"Like what?" He followed her shift of topic so quickly, she wondered if his thoughts had been on the same thing.

"I simply don't know." She added a plate to the pile of clean ones. "But there must be something."

"I suppose we could—I don't know. Maybe I could offer to fly her back to her parents wherever they are."

"If they'll have her back."

"Yes, there's that, isn't there?"

"Is there a place that takes unwed mothers?"

"It's never been a topic I explored."

"Me either."

He shrugged. "Doesn't seem to be any way for us to help."

He finished the dishes and turned to face her. "So you're finally willing to admit that a baby can't be held responsible for what happens."

She shook her head. "I know where you're going with this."

He grabbed her around the waist. "I'm sure you do. But humor me." He took her silence for acquiescence. "Isn't it time you stopped feeling like you're to blame for your mother's early death?"

She met his gaze without blinking, while inside, arguments raced through her mind.

"Let's take it a step further. Can you see you aren't responsible when things go wrong?"

"I don't think I am."

"Really? So whose fault was it when the wind blew down the clothesline?"

"I shouldn't have loaded it so heavily," she mumbled.

"Whose fault was it when the wash tub sprung a leak?"

She refused to meet his eyes.

"Who did you blame when Nellie had problems having her baby? Who did you blame when the doctor was out of town?"

She steadfastly refused to look at him. His arguments made her concerns sound silly.

"Grace, who did you blame when the engine on the airplane stalled and you lost our baby?" His low voice twanged with pain.

"I didn't blame you."

"No. You blamed yourself and figured you should have to pay. Do you know how much it hurt to watch you doing that?"

She met his pain-laced dark gaze for a moment and then let her gaze skid away. "When you say it like that, it makes my suffering sound childish."

He grabbed her hands, forcing her to meet his eyes. "I don't mean you shouldn't hurt because of the baby, nor that you shouldn't suffer. That's different. Blaming yourself is futile and destructive. It's as unfair as blaming Maggie Murphy's infant."

She searched his eyes, trying to sort out her confused

thoughts. Finally she shook her head. "It isn't that simple."

"Why not?"

"I can see it's foolish to blame myself for things I have no control over, but. . ." Her voice dropped to a strangled whisper. "What about the stupid things I do?"

His face serious, he shook her tenderly. "Grace, you are way too hard on yourself. No one is perfect. We all have to learn as we go along. Often we learn by doing things the wrong way first. That doesn't make you stupid—only human."

She let herself drown in his gaze. Slowly she nodded. "I suppose you're right. I'll try harder."

He shook his head. "Stop trying harder. It's enough to do what you can. And for my sake, have a little fun doing it."

"I have fun."

"Seems to me you always end up feeling guilty about it. Sometimes I think you feel you have to take your father's place. And Irene's."

"Whatever do you mean by that?"

He grinned crookedly. "Seems to me you had more fun when you lived at home. As if your father and Irene provided the 'shoulds' in your life, leaving you free to enjoy yourself. Now. . ." He shrugged. "It seems you're lost without their control. You try and replace them, and you're far harder on yourself than they were." He paused. "And you know as well as I do that they treated you like a fragile child." His smile grew tender. "You are not a child, and you're certainly not fragile. Why, you are the most self-sufficient, practical, independent woman I have ever been married to."

The tightness in her throat that promised tears dissolved in laughter. "You are so pitiful sometimes."

"Ah, but what would you do without me?"

She smiled up at him. "I couldn't."

He kissed her thoroughly.

As they prepared for bed, Grace's mind returned to Maggie Murphy and her child. "I can't get them out of my mind," she told Billy.

"I know. Perhaps someone will have already helped them."

Grace doubted it, but she didn't say anything more.

The specter of the huddled figure outside the closed door haunted Grace. Long after Billy's breathing deepened, she lay staring into the darkness. It wasn't right. Especially for that baby. There had to be something she could do to help. Perhaps there was. Long into the night, she worked out the details of a plan.

Over breakfast the next morning, she broached the subject with Billy.

"I think I know what we can do."

"About what?"

"About Maggie Murphy and her baby."

He nodded. "I wondered if you would forget about them. Go ahead. Tell me what you figured out."

She spent several minutes outlining her plan. He nodded several times and thought about it several minutes before he answered.

"It seems you've considered every possibility. Go ahead. Whatever you do has my full support."

She leaned over and kissed him. "Thank you, Billy."

"You'll be needing some money." He went to the bedroom and returned with a roll of bills. "I hope this is enough."

For the first time she wondered if she was doing the right thing. "This is most of our money, isn't it?"

"There's more where that came from."

She nodded, stuffing the bills in her handbag. "I'll get ready right away."

He waited while she gathered up things she needed, then walked her to the car and kissed her good-bye. "I'm proud of you, Grace," he whispered.

Her heart too full to speak, she waved as she sped away.

She drove slowly up and down the streets, not really expecting to see anything. Partway down the block, she turned into the alley, slowly going its length. Where would they go? An idea came, and she turned down the alley behind the hotel. Again, nothing.

Grace stopped the car to think. She'd need to find shelter and food. She turned down another alley. At first she couldn't see any possibilities, but then she saw the leaning shed at the back of the yard. She got out and listened. If she heard any-thing, it was only a cat meowing. Neverthe-less, it wouldn't hurt to check. She picked her way to the door hanging by one hinge, pushed it open, and peered into the dim interior. She saw the bundle of rags and the pale cheek of the woman and caught her breath. Perhaps she was too late.

She sprang to the limp form. Large, fever-bright eyes turned to her. She bit her lip. This was no woman, simply a young frightened girl who drew back at her approach.

"Don't be afraid. I've come to help."

The girl moaned.

"Are you Maggie Murphy?"

The girl blinked, and Grace took it for acknowledgment.

"Where is your baby?"

The over-bright eyes looked toward her swaddled arms.

Holding her breath, fearing what she would find, Maggie lifted the covers. The baby lay very still, eyes closed. Maggie waited. The tiny chest fluttered. "She's still alive," she mur-mured. Barely. She must act fast. But how to get this pair into her auto?

"Old Len," she muttered. "I'll be right back," she told Maggie.

Maggie closed her eyes.

Grace sensed the defeat.

"No. I will. I promise." But there wasn't time to argue. She dashed for the car and, driving fast, headed for the livery barn.

"Len," she called.

"Why, Mrs. Marshall. What can I do for you?"

"Can you come quickly? I need your help."

"Why sure. You can count on Old Len."

"You can come with me in the car."

He ambled out and climbed aboard. "I'm not too sure about these things." He nodded toward the car's bonnet.

'Seems to me you can count on a horse and wagon."

Grace smiled. "Billy says the same thing about machines."

"Where you taking me?"

Grace hesitated. What if he refused to help? She couldn't lift Maggie into the car without assistance. Yet if he wasn't going to help, he could as easily refuse there as here. She sighed. "I've found a young mother and her baby. They're very weak. They need help."

He nodded. "Young Maggie Murphy." He nodded again. "I'm right glad to hear someone has the gumption to help them."

Her breath gushed out. "Thank you, Len."

She drew to a stop beside the lean-to and hurried inside, Len at her heels. "I want to get her into my car."

"And then what?"

She jerked to a halt. "I thought of taking her to the hotel."

"Good idea."

Grace opened the cover and gingerly took the infant. The baby meowed a protest. Ignoring the alarm clenching her heart, Grace cradled the infant close.

Len nudged her aside. "I'll carry this wee thing to the car." He lifted Maggie like she was nothing. Maggie opened her eyes, saw the baby in Grace's arms, and sighing, let her eyes close again.

Len put Maggie on the seat, standing on the running board to hold her in place.

Grace nestled the baby beside Maggie, then drove to the hotel.

When she stopped, Len said, "I'll wait here until you get a room. I wouldn't be telling them why you want it, if I were you."

"I understand."

Inside, she waited for the gray-haired lady to turn from making entries in a large journal. "I'd like to rent a room."

"Certainly. Mrs. Marshall, isn't it?"

"Yes, it is." She handed the woman a bill and took the key, hurrying back outside. "Room seven," she told Len. "No questions asked."

"Then let's get them there right quick." He took Maggie in his arms and headed inside, Grace on his heels, carrying the infant.

The gray-haired woman glanced up. Her smile froze. She shot out of the chair. "Wait a minute. What do you think you're doing?"

Len marched forward without hesitation. Grace followed suit.

"You can't do this."

"Is there something wrong with my money?" Grace demanded in a firm voice.

The woman hesitated. "Of course not."

"Then I assume I can use the room as I choose."

"Let it go, Mrs. Spicer." Len's voice, though quiet, invited no argument.

Grace hid a smile as Mrs. Spicer's mouth dropped open, then clamped shut. "Humph," she muttered, turning back to the desk.

Upstairs, Len lay Maggie on the bed and gave Grace a worried look. "Are you wanting me to fetch Doc?"

Grace nodded gratefully. "I would really appreciate it."

Len left before she finished speaking.

Grace forced herself to look at the limp infant in her arms and heaved a relieved sigh when she detected movement in the tiny chest. "Hurry, Doc," she murmured as she wrapped the baby tighter, then placed it on the bed beside Maggie.

Her heart beat loudly in the silent room. Maggie moaned once without opening her eyes. Grace's lungs hurt. She reminded herself to breathe.

Hearing boots thudding up the stairs, she rushed to open the door. Len shepherded in Dr. Martin. Grace had never met him, but he didn't pause for formality, simply nodded and turned to the pair. "What do we have here?"

He examined the baby first. The infant opened her eyes and let out a weak wail. Doc shook his head. "I'd say she's lucky to have survived this long. She'll need lots of care if she's going to live."

"I'll do it," Grace said in a quiet, determined voice.

"You'll be needing milk and bottles and all the rest of the paraphernalia."

"I'll get it at the store."

Len stepped forward. "I'll do the running for you."

She shot him a grateful look.

"You'll need to clean her up. She still has birthing fluid on her. But be gentle. She's very weak. We'll start her on sugar and water and see how she does. Now if you two would step out a minute, I'll have a look at this poor girl."

Len and Grace waited in the hall. Grace barely dared to breath.

Doc stepped out, shaking his head. "We'll do our best, but I'll be frank. She's not in good shape. Rampant peritoneal infection, poor condition." He shrugged. "I'll send over some things." Grace listened carefully as he told her how to care for Maggie. He didn't have to tell her the first thing was a bath, the odor was telling enough.

Len left with Doc, promising to return with milk and the rest of the supplies Grace needed. "I'll tell Mrs. Spicer to send up several buckets of hot water as well."

Grace closed the door behind them. Her legs began to shake, and she leaned against the door for support. The enormity of the situation hit her. How was she to care for a sick baby and young mother?

A knock forced her to stand straight. A sturdy young girl held two buckets of hot water. "Mrs. Spicer said I should bring you these." She ducked her head.

"Thank you. Could you possibly bring me two more?"

"Certainly, Ma'am." The girl turned and fled.

Grace turned to the baby first, gently sponging the soil from her tiny body. "Poor wee mite," she crooned, shocked at how lifeless the limbs felt. "It will be a miracle if you survive." When she finished, she wrapped the baby in a clean towel.

Len returned with supplies from Doc. "He said the bottles

are sterilized. Said to try two ounces every two hours. Said to take care of the baby first, then tend to Maggie." He glanced at the girl on the bed. "Poor soul."

Heart quaking with uncertainty, Grace poured the warm sugar water into a bottle and screwed on the nipple. She cuddled the infant close as she had seen Nellie do and inserted the nipple. The baby gagged. Grace jerked the bottle out. "You must eat, little one. I can't let you die." Slowly, she tickled the little mouth with the nipple, smiling when the baby made sucking motions. Again she tried the nipple. The baby sucked weakly, then choked.

Her mouth suddenly so dry it felt like cotton, Grace flipped the baby over and patted her back. "Baby, you near frightened me to death. How am I ever going to get enough nourishment in you?" She tried again and again managed to get several swallows into the infant. Suddenly the baby fell limp. "You better not be dead," Grace muttered. "Not after I tried so hard to get you to eat." But she could see a faint rising and falling of the chest. She checked the bottle. "One ounce." It would have to do. There was still Maggie to care for.

"Let's get rid of these wretched rags," she muttered, pulling one arm out of a torn and dirty sleeve. Maggie opened her eyes long enough to give Grace an annoyed look and mutter something under her breath. "You could give a little aid," Grace said.

Maggie rolled over enough for Grace to slip her clothes off.

Grace filled a basin with warm water and the solution Doc had sent and scrubbed a layer of dirt off. Maggie's skin burned with fever. Despite the looseness of skin at her tummy, she was thin to the point of emaciation. Once or twice, Maggie opened her eyes and gave Grace a suspicious look.

Grace finished and threw a clean cover over Maggie.

A knock at the door made her jump.

"Who is it?"

"Len and my sister, Maude."

She threw open the door. Maude bustled in. "Len told me

all about it. I made some soup for the young lady and brought you some tea and sandwiches." Both she and Len had full hands. "Now let me see to the baby."

She plucked the infant up and tsked. "Not very good, is she? But not to worry. We'll do our best." She filled a fresh bottle and managed to get another ounce in while Grace ate a sandwich and drank a cup of tea.

"I'm so grateful," she murmured. "I didn't know how I'd manage to do everything."

Maude glanced up from feeding the baby. "You're a brave young lady. I admire your stand. It's time someone ignored the self-righteous old busybodies around town and showed a bit of Christian charity."

"It's nothing that heroic. I simply couldn't stand back and not do anything."

"Rightly so. Rightly so." Maude set aside the bottle. "That's all the wee mite is going to take for now. And we'll be grateful for small mercies, won't we?"

Grace met Len's eyes across the room and smiled at his wink.

Maude paid them no mind. "Let's see if we can do as well with the poor young mother." She shook her head. "Seems a whole lot too young to be a mother, I'd say."

"What's done is done," Len said.

"That's a fact. That's a fact," Maude agreed, opening a jar of delicious-smelling broth.

Grace helped her put another pillow behind Maggie's head.

"Now, Girlie, why don't you try some of my famous chicken soup? Good for what ails you."

"She'd say the same whether it was pneumonia or warts," Len muttered.

Grace giggled.

"And have I ever been wrong?" Maude demanded.

"Not so's you'd admit it." Grace caught the glint of humor in his eyes.

Maggie turned her head away when offered a spoonful, but Maude coaxed some into her.

"That will do for now, you poor child. You go ahead and sleep." As she tidied up, she gave orders. "There's more soup. Give her some every couple hours. And the same with the baby—sugar water every couple hours. I'll be back first thing in the morning, but if you run into trouble before that, you have Mrs. Spicer send for me." She paused to direct a word to Len. "You ready?"

"If you say so." He ambled for the door. "Good luck," he said to Grace as he shut it.

Maude's words carried to her. "She's going to be needing a whole lot more than luck. Plenty of hard work will be needed to get that pair up and about."

Grace smiled. Maude had been like a breath of fresh air—or maybe more like a brisk fall breeze.

Grace got little rest going from Maggie to the baby and back again, patiently trying to get each to take just one more swallow. As dawn turned the sky steel gray and then pink, sending faded light into the room, Grace stood and stretched.

"Who are you?"

She fair jumped out of her skin at the low words and jerked around to see Maggie's unblinking gaze upon her. "I'm Grace Marshall."

"Why're you helping me?" The look was both direct and suspicious.

"Because I want to."

"I got no money."

Grace smiled. "I didn't expect you would have."

Maggie closed her eyes as if searching inside for strength. "How's my baby?"

For a moment, Grace hesitated, but that direct gaze demanded an honest answer. "She's weak, but I'm managing to get a little sugar water into her."

"I figured she'd be dead by now." The words were flat, emotionless, but Grace caught the flash of pain that crossed her features.

"It must have been terrible."

Maggie didn't answer; her look indicated the answer was self-evident.

Doc came by to check the patients. "The baby is showing improvement. Keep up the sugar water every two hours." He shook his head as he looked at Maggie. "We'll do what we can."

Maude and Len followed on his heels, bringing fresh soup and sandwiches. Maude helped feed both patients, then left with the used dishes and bottles. "I'll boil these up and bring them back."

Silence fell. Grace leaned back in the chair.

"Mrs. Marshall?"

Grace hurried to Maggie's side.

"I know I'm getting weaker. I feel it in me." Maggie closed her eyes, her breathing ragged. "I want you to let my parents know about my baby."

Grace nodded. "Of course." She found a pencil and piece of paper. "Why don't you give me their names and address?"

Her voice weak and faltering, Maggie recited the information, then lay still. Thinking the young woman had fallen asleep, Grace rose.

"Wait," Maggie whispered, struggling to find the strength to continue. "If they won't take the baby, will you keep her?"

The enormity of the request made Grace's knees weak. How could this poor child think her parents would refuse to take her baby? To have no one to turn to but a stranger. She swallowed back the sting in her throat. "I would be honored."

Maggie thanked her with her eyes. "I want a lawyer to write it down."

Grace blinked. "Of course, whatever you want. I'll ask Len to send one next time he comes."

Maggie's head fell to the side.

Grace tiptoed away and prepared a bottle for the baby.

≈

Len and Maude came again that afternoon.

Grace told of Maggie's request for a lawyer.

"I'll see to it right away," Len offered.

"Could I get you to take a message to Billy as well? Tell

him what's happening and explain I'll be home when I can."

Len readily agreed.

The lawyer arrived and drew up papers as Maggie asked and had her sign them. He handed one set to Grace. "It's all legal and final. If the Murphys don't want this infant, she's yours, signed, sealed, and delivered."

Grace stared at the papers long after the lawyer had left. She hadn't even had time to consult Billy. What would he say?

Doc came again that evening.

"The baby is much stronger."

Grace knew it already. The child had taken two ounces in a rather greedy fashion.

"I think I'd like to keep her on the sugar water one more night," Doc said. "Our Maggie is failing though."

This also was not news to Grace. Maggie seemed to have spent her last bit of energy seeing the papers were duly drawn up and signed. Since then she had slipped farther and farther away.

"I'll be surprised if she lasts the night," Doc whispered. "Do you want me to send someone to stay with you?"

For a moment, Grace's old fears rushed headlong into her mind, and she wished she could be anywhere but here. But she shook her head. "I'll be fine." This was something she had to do.

She slept a little while Maude fed the baby, and then she was alone with the patients, the darkness shutting out everything but the two faces in the circle of light from the bedside lamp.

Maggie opened her eyes. Her mouth moved, but Grace couldn't hear what she said. She leaned closer.

"I want to see my baby."

Grace brought the sleeping infant to Maggie, holding her so Maggie could see her face.

Maggie again tried to speak. Grace bent close. "Kiss her for me every day." She gave the baby one last look. Already the light of life was fading from the too-wide eyes. Slowly, wearily, Maggie closed her eyes and sighed. A shudder rattled through her body, and then she was still.

Grace gently closed Maggie's eyes and folded her hands across her chest. She would send for Doc in a moment, but for now she wanted to be quiet and remember Maggie's last words.

"Kiss her every day for me."

Tears blurred Grace's vision as she gathered the baby to her bosom and kissed her soft cheek. "This is from your mommy," she whispered. She breathed deeply of baby scent. Poor Maggie. She hadn't even had a chance to name her wee daughter.

eleven

Grace didn't know how Billy knew to come, but he was there at her side when the doctor and undertaker came. A wire was sent to the Murphys, and when no reply came, Billy arranged the service at the graveside to which exactly four people attended, not counting the baby and the reverend.

Doc had been unable to come because of an urgent call from a patient, but he had patted Grace's arm before he left. "You take the little one home and continue doing what you've been doing. She'll soon settle and do just fine."

"I hope so." Grace couldn't help but be a little doubtful. The first time she'd given the baby milk, it had come up—she'd been about to say as fast as it went down, but remembering how she'd coaxed the baby to take two ounces, she changed her mind. It had come up all at once, sour smelling, soaking both the baby's nightie and Grace's last clean top.

Doc suggested diluting the milk with sugar water.

The baby kept it down better, but both Grace and baby bore the smell of spit-up. As the infant's strength grew, so did her lung power. Grace reminded herself that little Rebecca Deans fussed a lot too.

The reverend closed his Bible and stepped around the fresh grave. "God bless you for your kindness," he said to Maude and Len. Then he stood before Grace. "You've done a noble thing." He paused. "But there'll be people who don't approve."

Grace waited, wondering if he meant himself.

"You can count on my support."

"Thank you." It eased her mind to hear him say it.

He touched the baby's head and made a clucking noise. "It won't be easy for this one."

The baby screwed up her face and screamed.

Rev. Albright chuckled. "She's going to let the world know what she thinks about it. By the way, what's her name?"

"No one has given her a name yet."

"No wonder she's mad at the world. Give her a name. That will help."

Grace nodded, though she wondered what difference it would make to the squalling infant in her arms.

Billy put an arm around her and steered her toward the car. "Let's go home."

The movement of the car soothed the baby, and she slept.

"Have you thought of a name?" Billy asked.

Grace shook her head. "I thought of calling her Maggie after her mother but decided she'd have enough trouble escaping her past without branding her."

"How about Judy? I've always liked that name."

"Judy?" Grace rolled the name around in her mind. "I like it." She looked down at the sleeping infant. "Are we doing the right thing?"

Billy shrugged. "We're doing the best we can."

The best she could do seemed inadequate, Grace decided in the following days. Little Judy slept no more than an hour or two at the most.

One afternoon, Billy stretched out on the sofa, the baby on his chest, patting her incessantly. "This doesn't seem right. She pulls her knees up like she's in real pain."

Grace nodded, then wished she hadn't. She was so weary it hurt to move her head. "Nellie's baby fusses a lot too."

"But does she scream like this? Does she pull in her legs like this? Is her little tummy as hard as a rock?"

"I don't know." She prepared another bottle. "Doc said I was doing everything right. I don't know what else I should try." She thought for a moment. "Willow gave Nellie something that helped soothe the baby's tummy. Maybe you should go see what she can suggest."

Grace took the baby and sat in the rocking chair. The baby

took the bottle eagerly. Grace let her head fall back. "Maybe this time she'll settle."

Billy shook his head. "We've been saying that for two weeks now. It's time to see what else we can do. I'll go see Willow right away."

But he did better than go see Willow; he brought her back with him.

Willow took the crying baby from Grace's arms. "Ya got a fussy one, did ya?"

Grace nodded, so weary she felt she would never have the energy to smile again.

"I'll have a look at her." Willow stared down at the crying scrap of humanity for what Grace thought was an inordinately long time. Then she ran her fingertips over the baby's head, along her neck and down both sides of her stomach. She felt both legs. Her expression remained serious, almost stern.

Grace began to shiver. "What's the matter?"

Finally Willow turned, and what Grace saw in her friend's eyes made her heart clench.

"I can give ya some gripe water. Same as I did Nellie. Ya can give the baby a taste on her gums when she's fussing." Her gaze returned to the child.

Grace caught a glimpse of sadness, or was it fear? A tremor snaked down her spine. She'd wanted Willow to smooth her magical hands across the baby and say something easy, like put this herb in her bottle.

She'd wanted Willow to soothe away her fears. Instead, Willow looked like someone had handed her something smelly. "You don't blame the baby for who her mother was, do you?"

Willow looked surprised. "Of course not."

"Then what is it? I see something in your eyes. Tell me what it is."

Willow handed the baby to Grace. "Give her all the loving ya can."

The words held all the finality of a death sentence. Grace

cradled the baby to her breast. "She's just fussy. That's all. She'll outgrow it."

Willow nodded. "Perhaps."

Grace stared at her. Perhaps? Was it possible Judy had something wrong? But Doc had seen her only two days ago and said Grace was doing everything right. A suspicion leapt to her mind. Doc hadn't said anything about how the baby was doing. No, that wasn't correct. Doc had said the baby wasn't gaining.

Willow handed her a bottle. "Give her this no more than three times a day. It will help her sleep. Ya be sure and rest while she's resting." Her gaze lingered on the baby. "Sometimes it's for the best," she murmured, the words so soft Grace could almost believe she hadn't heard them.

Almost. But not quite.

She waited until Billy had taken Willow home again. She waited until little Judy had eaten again and had a few drops of Willow's concoction. She waited until the baby settled into a fretful sleep before she turned to Billy. "I'm not. . ." Her throat clogged with tears, and she clamped her teeth tight, pushing back the storm. "I. . ."

But she was helpless before the viciousness of her emotions. She flung herself into Billy's arms and wept until his shirt was soaked. Finally, her emotions spent, she pulled a hankie from her pocket and blew her nose.

"Gracie, what is it?" Billy's voice sounded strained.

She couldn't bear to leave the shelter of his arms nor to lift her ear from his chest where she heard the steady beat of his heart.

"What did Willow say?"

A shiver shook her insides. She forced a breath into the depths of her lungs. "It was more the way she looked. Then just before she left, she mumbled something about it being for the best." She pushed back so she could see Billy's face. "I don't think she meant me to hear her." She grabbed his damp shirtfront. "It was like she saw something. Something that made her act like. . ." Grace shuddered, swallowed hard, continued, her voice a strained whisper. "Like there was no hope for Judy."

Billy looked startled. His gaze darted to the other room where Judy slept. Then his jaw twitched, and hardness made his voice dark and brittle. "There must be something we can do. I'll get Doc first thing in the morning. He'll know what to do."

Nodding, she buried her face against his chest again. His arms held her with an urgency she knew wasn't for her. Billy was as shocked and dismayed by Willow's attitude as she.

Next morning, Billy and Grace explained their concerns to Doc. He nodded gravely and, ignoring Judy's screaming protest, examined every inch of the baby. He indicated Grace should dress Judy again while he folded his stethoscope and put it away.

Billy took Grace's hand as they waited for Doc to stop fiddling with his bag.

Finally, he looked at Billy. When he avoided meeting Grace's eyes, her legs turned rubbery, and she clung to Billy's hand, jiggling Judy, trying to quiet her so she could hear what Doc had to say.

"I've heard of cases like this, though I have never personally seen one before." He cleared his throat. "For whatever reason, some babies fail to thrive." His face puckered with wrinkles. He suddenly looked very old. "I can give you a tonic, but other than that, I don't know what else to suggest."

"Doc, are you saying there's nothing we can do?" Billy's voice crackled.

"Give her all the love you can." His gaze flickered to Grace, then back to Billy. "You both need to get all the rest possible. I can give you some pills to help you sleep if you like." He held a bottle out to Billy. Grace watched Billy's hand move woodenly to take it.

"Call me if you want anything. Anything at all."

Grace's heart beat loud enough to hear it above wee Judy's howls; she turned to face Billy, knowing her eyes showed the same distress his did.

The baby stopped crying, but Grace knew Judy was only catching her breath for another onslaught of screaming. In that one quiet moment, the sudden silence as loud as the baby's cries, wee Judy looked up at Grace, her dark blue eyes demanding. Pleading. At that moment, Judy was no longer a poor helpless baby needing love and care; she became a strong-willed person who made her way into Grace's heart with all the determination of a bull—or a hummingbird. Grace swallowed hard. *Heart of my hearts, sweet baby.*

She stroked the soft baby cheek with the back of her fingers. "Look at her, Billy. She has the heart of a fighter. She's begging us to help her." Barely able to speak past the tightness in her throat, she whispered hoarsely, "I won't let her. . ." She stumbled over the word shouting through her thoughts. Her mind rebelled at thinking it, let alone saying it. She found another word instead. "I can't let her go."

Billy pressed his balled-up fist to his mouth and shook his head. "I know. But I feel so helpless." He chewed his bottom lip and groaned. His expression tight, he drew Grace gently into his arms, Judy cradled between them. For a minute the baby stopped crying. She gave a loud hiccup and looked startled at the unusual noise coming from her.

Grace giggled. "I think she likes being squeezed between us."

Billy took the baby's hand. The wee fingers curled around his finger. "You hang on, little one. Just like that."

Grace met Billy's eyes. Silently she joined her heart with his in a vow to save this baby.

A troubled expression clouded his eyes.

"What's the matter?" she asked.

"This is going to be a tough battle." He searched her eyes. "One we might lose in the end if we believe what the experts say." His eyes darkened with concern. "You've already lost so much. Are you sure you're up to this?"

She laughed low in her throat. "I don't believe you. Aren't you the one who is always telling me I'm so capable? And now when I'm sure I can do something, you doubt me."

He grinned sheepishly. "I guess it sounded foolish. I only want you to understand clearly what we have ahead of us."

"I can do this."

"I know you can, but you won't be doing it alone. You heard Doc. We need to take care of ourselves." He smiled down at Judy, who wrinkled her face in preparation for another session of screaming. "If we don't, we won't be able to take care of this little missy. So from now on, as much as possible, we'll take turns walking this little one."

She nodded. A rest once in awhile would be good.

He took the squalling baby. "You look all in. You go have a sleep while I feed Judy. Maybe I'll take her for a drive so you can sleep without benefit of her singing."

Grace laughed. "Singing is it now? Who knows? Perhaps you're right. Perhaps she's starting early to practice for opera."

Billy shuddered. "Oh, please, not opera." He gave Grace a little shove. "Off you go to bed."

Day after day passed. Despite Billy's help, Grace knew exhaustion like she'd never imagined possible, exhaustion far more profound than physical fatigue. Despite their love and care, Judy continued to throw up almost as much as she drank. Her arms and legs were like twigs, they were so thin. It seemed ironic to put a nappy on her wasted buttocks.

"You go to church," Billy insisted one Sunday. "The break will do you good. Me and Judy will be all right for awhile." He bounced the fretting baby.

Grace drew back. "When did her screams become such weak whimpers?"

Billy shook his head. "She's getting weaker every day." He met her eyes. Her pain reflected in his dark gaze. "Go to church. Pray."

She turned on her heels and left the house. The cold wind immediately caught her breath. A dusting of snow filled the air. Winter would soon be upon them. She sighed. The cold, bareness of winter already filled her heart.

By the time she got to church, the sun stared bleary-eyed

through the thin clouds. She sat for a moment before she trudged inside, wishing she hadn't come. What she really needed was sleep. She could sleep a hundred years and not feel rested because, she admitted, sleep alone would not provide the refreshment she needed. Only Judy thriving would do that.

The hymns of faith mocked her. Where was God when they needed Him? Pray, Billy said. But she didn't know how to pray. Not for something like this.

Nellie waited for her at the end of the service, handing Rebecca to Tom as she took Grace's arm and led her away to a private corner of the room. "Grace, how is Judy? Not that I really need to ask. You look half dead."

Grace closed her eyes, pushing away nausea and exhaustion. Fear and worry plagued her like a persistent disease. She shivered. "I can't stand it much longer. Why should a poor helpless baby have to suffer so much? And we can't do anything about it."

Nellie hugged her.

"I'd give anything to be able to help her." The tortured words spilled from Grace's lips. "If only there was something."

"There's prayer." Nellie said it like nothing more was needed.

"Billy sent me to church to pray." Desperate for help from any source, Grace turned her face to Nellie. "But I don't know how to pray."

Nellie smiled sweetly. "You know how to talk, don't you?"

"Don't be silly." This was no time for frivolity.

"I'm not. What I'm trying to say is prayer is nothing more than talking—talking to God."

Grace stared at Nellie, her thoughts trapped by the simplicity of Nellie's statement. Finally, she shook her head. "You don't just waltz up to God and say, 'Hello there, I've something to say to You.'"

"But that's exactly what you do. That's part and parcel of the work Jesus did on the cross."

"I don't understand." A deep longing to believe sucked at Grace's insides.

"Didn't Jesus say believing on Him gave us the right to be children of God?"

Grace nodded.

"Think about it. Don't children go to their father in trust and faith, asking for things they need, telling about their dreams and desires?"

"It seems irreverent. Too easy."

Nellie gave her a gentle smile. "Sometimes we reason ourselves right out of the things God wants for us. I suggest you simply decide you have the right to talk to God about your fears and needs and then just do it. Stop waiting to try and figure out all the theological ramifications."

Grace nodded. "I'll try." Sighing, she wrapped the woollen kerchief around her hat and pulled on her gloves. "I must get home."

Nellie gave her another hug. "I pray for you several times a day. I confess I'm not sure how to pray, whether to ask God to heal that poor baby or to give you strength to nurse her through her short life." Nellie's voice thickened. "I pray for both, and I leave the choice of life or death in God's hands; He alone knows what is best."

Grace nodded, too choked to speak.

The wind had died down; a watery sun gave the landscape a flat appearance, the lack of shadows erasing bumps and dips in the road.

Grace thought of Nellie's words. Talk to God like a child to a father. She took a deep breath. "God, I'm not sure about this praying business. It seems altogether too bold to come to You with my problems, but I have nowhere else to go." Embarrassed at the sound of her thin words in the flat light, she stopped talking.

Trust. The word blared through her mind.

She jolted around to see if someone had ridden up unnoticed, but she was alone in the gray world.

Trust Me.

The words came from inside her head. Was it as simple as that? Maybe it was. But did she want to trust God? Like Nellie said, He had the power of life and death. She rebelled at the idea of Judy dying.

Rebel or trust.

She could ask God to make Judy better, but was that trust?

She gripped the steering wheel so hard her hands hurt. Trust, she knew, meant leaving the choice with God. But she couldn't go on fighting God for this child. Her weariness was too bone numbing.

"God, I can only do as Nellie does: beg You to make Judy well, ask You to give Billy and me strength to nurse her and. . ." Her heart clenched painfully. "I leave the choice in Your hands." The words ended in a sob.

She drove on, not thinking, not feeling.

At home, she sat in the car a moment, then trudged indoors.

Billy lay on the sofa, one arm holding the weak baby, the other thrown over his eyes. He breathed deeply.

She tiptoed over and looked at Judy. The baby's eyes were open; she seemed to be staring at something a few inches away, then her face screwed up in pain.

Agony shot through Grace's body at what this poor child had to endure. "Poor baby," she crooned, taking the infant from Billy's chest, hoping to make it to the kitchen before Judy's wailing woke him. He lifted his arm and opened one eye. "Go back to sleep," she said. "I've got her."

He sighed wearily, closing his eye when he saw Judy in Grace's arms.

She warmed a bottle for Judy, enjoying the few minutes' peace that feeding provided. Judy wrapped her hand around one of Grace's fingers; she locked eyes with Grace, not blinking the whole time she sucked.

The feeling she had for this wee child was more intense than anything she could have imagined. "I love you, Baby," Grace murmured. "I want nothing more in the whole world than for you to get better, but I know how much pain you have to endure." Tears blurred her vision. "Ahh," she moaned. "I don't want to see you suffer anymore."

She checked the bottle. One ounce gone. Despite Judy's hunger, she didn't dare let her take more than that without burping, and she slipped the bottle away.

Judy smacked her lips and lay content.

"If only it could be like this." But experience told Grace otherwise. She wrapped Judy in the soft pink blanket, a gift from Nellie when they brought Judy home, and held the baby to her shoulder, patting her back until she burped.

The baby took another ounce. Grace cuddled her, tears trickling down her cheek.

Billy tiptoed in, leaning over to watch Judy resting against Grace's breast.

"This is the way it should be," he whispered.

She raised her teary gaze to him. "I know." Even as she spoke, Judy jerked her legs up, twitching in pain, and wailed. "Shh, shh." Grace rocked hard, knowing it did more to comfort her than it did Judy.

"How was church?" Billy asked above the wails.

"Have you noticed how we manage to carry on a conversation above her crying?"

Billy grinned. "If we didn't, we'd never speak to each other anymore."

She gave a shaky laugh. "Church was good." She sorted through her thoughts. "Nellie said she prayed for us every day." She explained how Nellie's prayers left the choice in God's hands.

Billy nodded. "It would be foolish to think we had any other option."

"What do you mean?"

"The choice is ultimately and finally God's as to when and who dies."

"Yes, but—"

"I know. We can fight it, but really we can't change it."

"Is that where trust comes in?"

His brows furrowed. "What do you mean?"

"I want to be able to pray and tell God to make her live." She turned her gaze to the distressed baby. "But I can't stand to see her suffer like this day after day." She lifted her face to Billy. His eyes glistened with tears. "So I have to choose to trust God to do what's best."

He nodded.

She went on. "I'm at my wit's end. I'm tired and discouraged. And I don't know how to cope. Nellie said to pray. You said to pray. But I've never prayed for anything for myself before. My prayers have been confined to the sinner's prayer—you know, 'Father, I have sinned, I know my sin keeps me from You. But Your Son, Jesus, by His shed blood, will cleanse me if I but ask.' And of course, I joined in praying for world peace during the war." Suddenly it seemed urgent for Billy to understand how she prayed on the trip home. "Today, driving home, I talked to God. I told Him I was willing to accept His choice regarding Judy." She paused, trying to understand this new sense of peace she felt. "I think I can accept whatever happens—not that I won't care. But somehow I know I can leave it with God."

Billy leaned his elbows on the table. "I'm glad for you, but the idea of Judy. . ." He coughed, unable to finish his sentence. "I'm afraid it makes me angry."

She nodded. "Things will work out. Isn't that what you're always telling me?"

He jerked to his feet. "Will they?" He stomped from the house.

A few minutes later he came to the door and called. "The weather has cleared. I'm going flying for a bit."

She listened for the sound of his plane as it took off and faded into the distance, then she rose and headed for the bedroom. He would have to find his own way of dealing with the situation.

She curled up on the bed. Judy seemed to crave the warmth and touch of another body, and so she settled the baby close to her, pulled a quilt around them, and tried to rest, dozing in between patting Judy. The little tyke fussed less than usual. Grace acknowledged the baby simply did not have the strength left to react to her pain.

When Grace awoke to Judy's wails, it was dark. She jumped out of bed, grabbed up the baby, and raced through the house. Empty. She flung the door open. No airplane. Judy kicked weakly. As Grace filled a sterile bottle and warmed the weakened milk, her limbs shook so bad, she spilled some.

Billy had not returned.

twelve

Hoofbeats thudded outside. Boots clattered on the step. "Mrs. Marshall?"

She clutched Judy closer. "Who is it?"

"Mr. Tunney sent me with a message."

Her nerves tightened. "Come in."

A gangly youth stepped in, his face ruddy from his ride in the cold. He yanked the ear-flapped hat from his head. "Mr. Tunney said I should tell you right away."

Time stopped at that instant. She nodded.

"Mr. Marshall phoned. He said not to worry. He had to take someone to the hospital in Calgary. He said he'll be home in the morning and tell you all about it." The boy twisted his hat. "That's all."

Grace smiled, her relief so great she felt weak. "Thank you. Do you want to warm up before you go back?"

"No, thank you, Ma'am. I'll be on my way."

She smiled at Judy. "He's fine," she whispered to the baby. "Aren't we glad?"

❧

Billy climbed from the cockpit, reached down, and pulled out a box. He waited until Grace stood beside the plane and handed her the box. "I think I've found the answer."

"Hello to you too. Glad to hear you missed me as much as I missed you."

He laughed. "You'll forget that when you see what I brought." He reached into the plane for two large bottles of water.

"Water? I should be excited about water?"

He jumped down, gave her a hurried peck on the cheek, and practically ran to the house. "I can't wait to try this."

He put the bottled water on the table and took the box

from Grace's arms, ripping it open and pulling out a pint of murky white liquid. "We're to mix it half-and-half with distilled water."

"And what will we have when we do?" She gave him a narrow-eyed look. "You are acting mighty strange."

"It's a special milk for Judy."

Her thoughts skidded to a halt as she stared at the jar in his hands. "Where did you get it?"

"I met a doctor at the hospital. He's been working on this for a long time. Where's a clean bottle?" He washed his hands as she got one out.

Slowly, carefully, he poured in one ounce of the milk and one ounce of water, then warmed the bottle. "I hear Judy fussing. Is it time for her to eat?"

Grace wrinkled her nose. "Isn't it always?" A two-hour schedule left time for little else.

"Get her. I'm going to feed her this."

Grace hovered close as Billy teased Judy to try the milk.

The baby turned away.

"She doesn't like it."

"The doctor said she wouldn't at first but to keep trying until we got some in her." He persisted.

Judy swallowed, whimpered a protest, then, too weak to fight him, sucked the bottle.

"Poor baby, she can't understand why it doesn't taste like it's supposed to." Grace held one little hand.

"The doctor says we won't know for at least forty-eight hours if this works." He turned from watching the baby to meet Grace's eyes. "He said he's seen cases like this, and he's found it's often due to cow's milk. He says many of these babies do well if you can find something else for them. Sometimes goat's milk works but not always, so he's worked on this special milk. He says he's seen several babies miraculously begin to thrive." Billy's eyes were dark, so intense she blinked before his gaze. "Maybe." His voice was low and deep. "Maybe we'll get a miracle."

She clung to his gaze. Did she dare hope?

"By the way, how did you find this doctor?"

"I forgot to tell you what happened."

"Yes, you did."

"When I left yesterday, I had no plans. I needed time to think."

She nodded. "I knew that."

"I flew over a farm southwest of here. Someone jumped up and down and waved at me. I could see several people clustered in the yard and thought I'd circle around and drop down. You know, give them a bit of excitement. But they didn't wave like they were being friendly. I thought maybe they needed something, so I dropped in. Here if the dad hadn't been gored in the chest by a bull. He was in pretty rough shape. I told them I would fly him to Calgary, so we loaded him up with a compress to his chest and away we went."

"How is he?"

"They sewed him up and said he'd live." Billy puffed out his chest. "The doctor said I saved his life."

"And it was this doctor who told you about the special milk?"

"No. I was hanging around, waiting to see what happened, and this orderly came along, and we started chatting. When I told him about Judy, he got all excited. 'There's a doctor here who can help you.' And he went and fetched this special baby doctor. Dr. Childs."

Grace giggled.

"Don't laugh; that was really his name."

She sobered. "I don't care what his name is. Do you really think he can be right about the milk?"

His look intense and dark, he said, "Didn't we pray for God to help?"

She nodded. "I decided to trust God. But I thought that meant accepting. . ." Her shoulders slumped forward. "I'm almost afraid to believe this can be the answer."

"We should know in a couple of days."

It was the longest two days she'd ever lived, longer than

when Billy was away in the war, longer than the trip west.

Wednesday night they went to bed to the sound of Judy's fussing.

"Does she seem any better to you?" Grace asked.

"She hasn't thrown up as much, has she?"

Grace tried to think. "I guess not."

"She's certainly no worse."

"No, she's no worse."

Exhausted, Grace fell asleep.

It was dark and cold when she wakened, wondering what had startled her from her sleep.

She lay listening.

Suddenly, she shot up in bed.

"What is it?" Billy was instantly awake.

"Listen. Do you hear Judy?"

They bolted out of bed, racing to the cradle in the front room. Billy lit the lamp, and they leaned closer.

Grace hardly dared breathe.

Billy's breath escaped in a gust. "She's sleeping." He lifted the lamp and looked into Grace's eyes. "I think it's working."

The next few days, the difference in Judy was nothing short of astounding.

"I believe in miracles," Billy said, watching the baby lay content after her feeding. His voice thickened. "I will thank God every day for sending one our direction." He chuckled. "I'll have to remember to thank Dr. Childs as well."

Grace knew peace like she'd never known. "I think I love her all the more for the struggle we've been through. She's a real fighter, isn't she?"

"She's a winner, for sure."

❧

Grace looked up from mending one of Judy's nightgowns. "I want to send her grandparents a picture of her." Judy's limbs had begun to fill out. "She has the most precious smile."

Billy bounced the baby on his knee. "Her whole nature is sunny. Maybe she got all the crankiness out of her system those first couple of months."

Judy laughed aloud, a burbling sound of pure joy.

Grace smiled. "No one would know this is the same child who lay whimpering and complaining two months ago." She rubbed the baby's head. "Her hair is coming in almost white. She didn't get that from either of us."

Billy laughed. "You sound like you've forgotten she didn't get anything from either of us."

"Apart from tons of love."

She took Judy to town the first warm day and had her picture taken. She sent one copy to the address Maggie had given them with a short letter telling about Judy.

And then she went home to prepare for Christmas.

"She'll love Christmas."

"I'm making her a toy train," Billy said.

"I'm making her a rag doll."

Exactly one week before Christmas, a wire arrived for the Marshalls. Everyone in town knew about it and speculated as to its contents.

The same lad who delivered messages for Mr. Tunney rode to the Marshall house to deliver it. Later he described how he'd waited while Mr. Marshall tore it open. The man's face had turned as white as milk, and without saying good-bye or thank you to the boy, he'd called for his wife.

"Grace, come here."

Grace heard the strain in his voice and dropped her sewing to hurry to the kitchen. "Billy, what's the matter?" His face was colorless.

"They're coming to get her."

"What are you talking about?" She took the yellow sheet of paper in his hands and felt the blood drain from her own face as she read the words.

She grabbed a chair and forced her knees to bend so she could sit. "Why now?"

Billy shook his head. "It must be the picture you sent."

"You mean they saw how cute she was and decided she was

worth keeping?" She couldn't keep the bitterness from her voice. "Where were they when she cried day and night? I wonder if they would have wanted her then." Her throat tightened. "I should have never sent them a picture."

Billy's head sank into his hands. "It's too late to worry about it. They do have the right to claim her."

She glanced again at the telegram. "They'll be here tomorrow."

They sat in shocked silence.

"I don't suppose we can run away?" Billy mumbled.

She giggled, the sound harsh. "We could fly up north."

But she knew they couldn't. And Billy knew it too.

They sat up late, taking turns holding Judy, keeping her awake as long as they could so they could see her blue, knowing eyes, so they could see her wide smile and hear her gurgling chuckle. But Judy liked her sleep and nodded off in Grace's arms.

"I can't imagine not having her," Grace whispered. "After all we've been through together, she's more than a baby—someone else's baby. She's a part of me. We've fought together until I feel like we've become one."

Billy nodded. "I feel the same way. But what choice do we have?"

"Choice. That word again. I remember when I said I would submit to God's choice, but when she got better I thought He had given me the better choice." A spasm shook her insides. "I never thought we would lose her this way."

Billy sat deep in thought. "I never told you what I decided when I was out flying that day I ended up in Calgary."

She waited, knowing he was collecting his thoughts.

"At that point I guess we both thought she was going to die."

Remembering that desperate time, Grace pressed her lips tight, tears choking her throat.

"You seemed to have come to grips with it. Like you say, you decided to trust God about it." He shook his head. "I struggled with that. First, we lost our own baby, and now, no matter what we did, it seemed we were going to lose this baby as well. It didn't seem fair."

He had a faraway look in his eyes as he recalled the experience. "But I was so tired of fighting the inevitable. I finally shouted as loud as I could, 'How can I fight You, God? How can I trust a God who lets babies die?' Nothing happened." He grinned sheepishly. "I guess I expected God to say sorry, or show me a glimpse of the future so I could trust Him. 'Course if you see the future, there is no need to have faith, is there?"

She didn't respond, wanting to hear how his questions had been resolved, for his contentment had been evident since his return. Or was it only that Judy had improved after that?

"I had decided I had no choice but to trust God." He snorted. "Some kind of trust that is—no other choice. But when Dr. Childs gave me that case of milk, I knew I had to trust God no matter what happened. Remember, I didn't know yet if it was going to work." He fell silent.

After several minutes, he added, "What a miracle that God provided the answer. He taught me to walk with Him even when I can't see what lies ahead. I guess now is the time to prove that truth in my life."

She nodded. "I tell myself the same thing, but it's so hard to think of losing her." Scalding tears raced down her cheeks.

He knelt before her, cradling the baby between them. "It's hardest to trust when the way looks dark."

"I know," she managed to whisper through her tears.

❧

Billy left Grace at home with Judy when he went to meet the train.

"This will be my last chance to have her to myself," Grace whispered, her throat too tight to speak normally.

"I feel like leaving them standing on the platform, but I suppose they would simply hire someone to bring them out."

He pulled her into his arms with a desperation matching

her own. She clung to him. He pressed his face to her hair, his breathing ragged, a moan rumbling in his chest.

"I've got to go." He hurried to the car without a backward glance.

She dressed Judy in a clean nightie and a pink sweater set. Judy gurgled and laughed, grabbing at the strings on the sweater, reaching for the bootees Grace put on her feet.

Tears blurred Grace's vision and hampered her attempts to get the active limbs into sleeves. Finished, she lifted the baby so she could look into her face.

"They will fall in love with you the minute they see you." Her voice shook. "I know it's for the best. You should be with your own people, but I will miss you so very, very much." She buried her face in Judy's neck. How she'd miss the sweet scent of the baby, the warmth of her body cuddled against her, and the pleasure of her smile.

All too soon she heard the return of the car. She would not go to meet them. She'd wait until they stepped into the house. Two extra minutes.

Billy pushed the door open, followed by a woman who bore a striking resemblance to Maggie and a dignified man in a heavy coat and bowler hat. Their glances barely touched Grace when Billy introduced her. Both of them dropped their gaze to Judy.

Mrs. Murphy hurried across the room. "So this is Maggie's baby."

"Judy, meet your grandmother," Grace murmured, forcing herself to release her grasp on the baby so the older woman could take her. She held her with the confidence of experience, her husband hovering close.

"She has Maggie's eyes," Mr. Murphy said.

"See that look in her eyes? She's very much like Maggie." The older woman dashed away a tear. She turned to Grace. "Do you mind if I sit?"

"Please do. I'm sorry. Forgive my poor manners. You too, Mr. Murphy."

They sat close together, facing Grace. "I understand you cared for Maggie her last few days. Tell us about it," Mrs. Murphy said.

The dark pain in the older woman's eyes melted Grace's reserve. "My condolences at the loss of your daughter." Her eyes lingered on Judy; she couldn't imagine losing this little one who had been a part of her life for a few months, how much more it would hurt to lose her years from now.

"She was brave to the last. Her biggest concern was to make sure proper arrangements were made for Judy." Grace told them of Maggie's last days. "She proved to be a real fighter. Judy seems to have inherited that same spirit." Grace told of Judy's early months.

Mr. Murphy blew his nose; his wife wiped her eyes with a monogrammed hankie. "If only we'd known."

Grace darted a look at Billy. It was he who voiced her thoughts. "I sent you a wire."

The older couple gaped at him.

"When Maggie died. When you didn't reply, we took care of arrangements."

Mr. Murphy's expression hardened. "We never got it." He gave his wife a steady look.

"Michael," she grunted, turning to explain to Grace. "Michael is Maggie's brother. He has an unforgiving spirit. He must have gotten the telegram and, knowing we would come, destroyed it without telling us."

Mr. Murphy struggled with his emotions. "Thank the good Lord for people like yourselves to help her and the baby."

"Taking care of Judy has been our greatest pleasure." Grace spoke with quiet dignity.

Mrs. Murphy touched her hand. "I'm so sorry to repay your kindness by taking the baby. I know it must hurt unbearably."

Grace nodded. "I've prepared tea."

Over tea, Grace told them about Judy's care and the special milk. "We have it shipped from Calgary." She gave the

name of the doctor. "You'll have to contact him to arrange to
have it delivered." But they lived south of Calgary, so it
shouldn't be a problem.

She could tell the couple was anxious to be on their way. "I'll
get the rest of Judy's things." They were already packed in a
cardboard suitcase in the bedroom. She hurried to get it, lingering to shed a few tears in private. Blankets and bonnet were
ready for the trip to town, but in the end, Grace kept the little
pink blanket she'd used so many times when rocking Judy.
She held it to her face and breathed the sweet familiar scent of
the baby who was about to be taken from her.

"Thank you, my dear." Mrs. Murphy took the blankets. "I
promise I'll keep in touch. We'll tell Judy about the people
who saved her life twice in a few months."

Grace nodded, her throat too tight to speak.

Billy stood waiting to leave. She knew he wanted to get
this over with as soon as possible.

Mr. Murphy cleared his throat. "Can I ask one last favor?"

Billy nodded.

"Could you show us where Maggie is buried?"

"I'll take you there before we go to the station."

Grace bent to give Judy one last kiss. When the baby
smiled, Grace could no longer restrain her tears. They flowed
unchecked down her cheeks as she bid farewell.

Billy hurried out. She knew he was having difficulty con-
trolling his emotions as well.

The door closed behind them. Grace sat at the table, her
face in her arms, and sobbed.

Somehow they made it through that night and the days
that followed. The house echoed with its silence. Grace wandered aimlessly, wondering how she'd kept busy before she
had Judy to care for.

Nellie sent a note inviting them to spend Christmas with
her, Tom, and Rebecca.

"Do you want to?" Billy asked.

"Not really. I'm not ready to see Rebecca yet." She paused.

"Unless you want to."

"I'd as soon stay home."

Billy spent long hours in the barn. Grace knew he was dealing with his sorrow in his own way.

They had packaged up Judy's gifts and sent them with her grandparents.

Christmas was quiet. Grace had knitted socks for Billy; he bought her a pair of warm winter boots. "So you can drive without freezing your feet."

Winter settled in with a vengeance after that. Snow blanketed the earth, muting colors and sounds. Grace, having discovered how much she enjoyed knitting, made two more pairs of socks, a pair of mittens, and then began a sweater for Billy.

Spring arrived in a warm chinook the last day of February. Within a week, all that remained of the snow was dirty drifts along the north side of the building and in the trees.

Billy got several calls for work. He flew supplies to a ranch camp. He took a friend of Mr. Boushee's out to the Turner Valley oil fields. Dr. Childs phoned a message for him to take some of the special milk to a family in northern Alberta.

One spring day, Grace walked out to the barn to find Billy. She carried Judy's pink baby blanket with her.

"You doing anything important right now?" she asked him.

"No, only tinkering. What did you want?"

"Could you take me flying?"

He dropped the pliers and stared at her. "You want to go up in the air?"

She giggled at his surprise. "I believe that's what flying entails."

His mouth dropped. He closed it, gulped, and stammered, "But I thought you would never go up again. After last time."

"There's been a lot of water under the bridge since then."

His eyes watchful, he nodded. "That's a fact."

"Well, yes or no?"

He grabbed a rag and wiped his hands. "Sure. Right now?"

"Seems as good a time as any." She enjoyed seeing his confusion. Not often she managed to have that effect on him.

"Right. *Gracie Two* is ready and waiting."

He helped her into the front compartment, and they roared into the sky.

The wind tugged at her skin, clear, fresh wind laden with the smell of melting snow and burgeoning life. Grace sucked in air, greedy for its cleansing taste. She looked down on the bare trees, the brown mottled ground, the roof tops.

The pink blanket lay next to her heart where she'd stuffed it inside her blouse. She pulled it out, unfolded it, and held it high overhead like a pink flag. It fluttered and caught the wind, tugging at her arm.

"Fly, Baby, fly," she called and let the blanket go, looking over her shoulder to watch it blow away. "Good-bye," she murmured.

Billy banked the plane in a sharp turn so they could watch the pink scrap. The wind filled it like a parachute, then it collapsed and drifted slowly downward, lazy and free, disappearing somewhere over the trees along the river.

Billy brought them back home.

He jumped out and reached for Grace, helping her to the ground.

"What was that all about?"

She struggled to find the right words. "I suppose you could say it was hello and good-bye."

His dark eyes demanded a better explanation.

"Good-bye to Judy, of course, but hello to the rest of my life." She laughed as joy bubbled inside her. "Remember when you talked about trust being for the times when we can't see or understand?"

He nodded.

"I've decided it's time to trust God, to leave the future in His hands and embrace the wonders of each day."

Billy grabbed her hand. "I've something to show you."

She followed him to the barn, where he pulled a rag off a square piece of wood.

"I spent the winter doing this."

She gasped. He had carved a beautiful picture of a garden full of bushes—wild Alberta rosebushes. Rosebushes with one bud and one open flower. Under the bud was the name Eleanor May; under the flower, Judy.

"It's beautiful. I didn't know you could do this sort of work."

"I didn't either." He ran his fingers along the names. "See how these are the only roses yet?"

She nodded, her eyes lingering on each name.

"And see how there's room for more blossoms on these bushes?"

Understanding his meaning, she lifted her face to him. "Billy, that is so special. Is it any wonder I love you so much?"

He leaned the carved picture against the wall so he could take her in his arms. "I love you too, Gracie." He kissed her.

He'd said the words she needed to hear, and they sang straight to her overflowing heart. Somewhere, somehow, when she wasn't watching or waiting for it, love had found a home in her. Love that poured out rather than waited, afraid and quivering, for someone to give it life. Love straight from the heart of God. He'd answered her prayers above and beyond what she'd dreamed possible.

She pulled back. "And maybe, just maybe—because it's too early to be certain—you might need to be carving another flower this fall."

"Another baby?"

"I think so."

He grinned so wide, she laughed. "Is it any wonder I love you, Gracie?"

"Because I make babies?"

"No. Because you are so full of lovely surprises. Because you have a beautiful personality. And because of the faith that has grown in you."

He is right, she thought. Life was full of surprise. Perhaps the biggest one of all was the discovery of her capacity to love despite the risks and pain. With God's help, she knew she could face whatever the future would bring.

A Letter To Our Readers

Dear Reader:

In order that we might better contribute to your reading enjoyment, we would appreciate your taking a few minutes to respond to the following questions. We welcome your comments and read each form and letter we receive. When completed, please return to the following:

Fiction Editor
Heartsong Presents
PO Box 719
Uhrichsville, Ohio 44683

1. Did you enjoy reading *Grace* by Linda Ford?
   ❑ Very much! I would like to see more books by this author!
   ❑ Moderately. I would have enjoyed it more if

   _____

   _____

   _____

2. Are you a member of **Heartsong Presents**? ❑ Yes ❑ No
   If no, where did you purchase this book? _____

   _____

3. How would you rate, on a scale from 1 (poor) to 5 (superior), the cover design? _____

4. On a scale from 1 (poor) to 10 (superior), please rate the following elements.

   _____ Heroine   _____ Plot
   _____ Hero   _____ Inspirational theme
   _____ Setting   _____ Secondary characters

5. These characters were special because?_____

_____

_____

6. How has this book inspired your life?_____

_____

_____

7. What settings would you like to see covered in future
   Heartsong Presents books? _____

_____

_____

8. What are some inspirational themes you would like to see
   treated in future books? _____

_____

_____

9. Would you be interested in reading other **Heartsong
   Presents** titles? ❏ Yes ❏ No

10. Please check your age range:
    ❏ Under 18   ❏ 18-24
    ❏ 25-34   ❏ 35-45
    ❏ 46-55   ❏ Over 55

Name_____

Occupation _____

Address _____

City_____ State_____ Zip_____

HIGHLAND
Legacy

4 stories in 1

*f*our generations of love are rooted in Scotland. When Audrey MacMurray seeks her Scottish roots, she uncovers the lives of brave, romantic women during the 1300s, 1700s, and 1800s. Authors include: Tracey V. Bateman, Pamela Griffin, Tamela Hancock Murray, and Jill Stengl.

Historical, paperback, 352 pages, 5 ³/₁₆"x 8"

❤ ❤ ❤ ❤ ❤ ❤ ❤ ❤ ❤ ❤ ❤ ❤ ❤ ❤ ❤

❤ ❤ ❤ ❤ ❤ ❤ ❤ ❤ ❤ ❤ ❤ ❤ ❤ ❤ ❤

Presents

Great Inspirational Romance at a Great Price!